NIG

FAN MAIL

Nicole Davidson

HarperCollins*Publishers*

First published in the USA by Avon Books in 1993
First published in Great Britain in 1996
by HarperCollins*Publishers* Ltd.,
77-85 Fulham Palace Road, Hammersmith, London W6 8JB

1 3 5 7 9 8 6 4 2

Copyright © Kathryn Jensen 1993
Published by arrangement with the author
ISBN 0 00 675257 8

The author asserts the moral right to be identified
as the author of the work.

Printed and bound in Great Britain by
Caledonian International Book Manufacturing Ltd,
Glasgow G64

To Bill,
a star in my book!

N. D.

Chapter 1

Christina English clutched the arms of her chair as a frightened whimper escaped from her lips. She felt totally alone in the darkness, abandoned by her friends. The air smelled of stale food and was sickly sweet, as if something had crawled under her seat and died there.

Closing her eyes, she swallowed. She counted her own heartbeats. When she reached ten, she forced herself to open one eye . . . then the other.

At first she saw nothing.

Then a raspy, panting sound alerted her that she had company.

A creature, possibly seven feet tall and easily as wide as a refrigerator, loomed out of the darkness. Green slime oozed from a wound in its breast where a knife had pierced its armor-like scales.

Pressing back into the seat cushion defensively, Christina bit down on her lower lip to keep from screaming and stared helplessly at the glowing monster. The knife hadn't slowed the thing down; it had only made it more angry.

Eyeing her, it plodded forward on immense, clawed feet. Closer. Closer it came, snarling and gnashing powerful teeth, the blood of its earlier victims still dripping from its jaws.

Something brushed against Christina's arm, and she let out a nerve-shredding scream.

"Randi!" she choked out. "Don't *do* that!"

"I—I'm sorry . . . I thought you might want some more popcorn."

Christina glared at the cardboard tub her girlfriend held out to her in the movie theater.

"How can you eat at a moment like this!" she hissed.

Randi Baxter shrugged. "I guess I just don't take horror flicks as seriously as you." Thrusting a fistful of buttery kernels into her mouth, she munched happily.

Christina turned back to the screen in time to see a young actress swing a machete and lop off the monster's head. Green blood gushed everywhere. But the creature still plodded forward, raking the air with deadly claws.

"Oh, gross!" Christina groaned, covering her eyes.

Five minutes later the movie was, thankfully, over. The swamp fiend had effectively wiped out more than half the cast in the goriest ways imaginable before the hero finally destroyed it with the help of a hefty supply of dynamite sticks. Everyone in the audience seemed to think *Lost Lagoon III* was a great flick.

"Weren't you even a little scared?" Christina asked as she followed Randi up the aisle toward the exit.

"Not really. I guess I'm too rational. I know things like that don't exist, so they can't scare me. Horror films are sort of silly, I think."

Christina sighed. Silly or not, she felt as if she'd been dragged through a mine field.

"Got any more popcorn?" she asked, as the crowd inched up the aisle. "I'm starving."

Randi glanced guiltily over her shoulder. "Sorry, it's all gone. Anyway, why did you want to see this movie? After the last horror movie we saw together, you didn't sleep for three nights."

"I know. And I won't sleep tonight either," Christina admitted with a sigh. "But *Lost Lagoon III* is Theodore Dreising's latest film."

"Dreising . . . the director?"

"Yeah," Christina said thoughtfully as they stepped through the exit into a soft spring night.

They crossed the parking lot, and she unlocked her car door. "There was a message from my manager on my answering machine this afternoon when I got home from school," Christina continued. "A New York agent contacted her this morning. Dreising plans to shoot his next movie in Connecticut, just twenty miles from here, and his casting director will be in New Haven next week to audition local talent for minor roles."

Randi stared at her over the roof of Christina's pink VW. "And you think you might get a part?" she gasped, her brown eyes as big as the Bug's shiny hubcaps.

"It's a long shot . . . but who knows." Christina ducked into the driver's seat, still talking as Randi hurried to climb into the passenger side. "Marsha says that only one part has been cast so far . . . the lead. Rumor has it that it'll be Kurt Richmond."

"Kurt Ri—" Randi squealed, pretending to swoon in her seat. "You're kidding! He's gorgeous . . . more than gorgeous. You mean, he and I are going to be in the same state? I'll die if I don't get to meet him . . . no, forget that." She glanced down at her plump middle. "I'll die if he sees me like this. How can I lose thirty pounds in a week?"

Christina laughed. "Relax. Movie gossip is hardly ever true. Richmond's never done a horror film. He starred in that Western with a bunch of his Brat Pack buddies from Hollywood and did a couple of romantic comedies—"

"Oh," Randi sighed as Chris pulled out of the parking lot, "I just *loved* him in *Last Embrace*."

3

"That was the only serious film he's done. It was pretty good."

"*Pretty* good?" Randi objected. "He was fantastic!"

"That's not what the critics said," Christina stated.

"Oh, dunk the critics in a swamp! What do they know? I think he's the most talented hunk ever."

"You're not sounding very rational now," Christina teased.

But she had to admit that thousands of teenage girls across the United States agreed with Randi. Kurt Richmond was the hottest teen sex symbol, even if he wasn't the best actor. Every one of his films had grossed millions of dollars, making him and his studio very, very rich.

But as a young actress herself—although admittedly one without film credits—Christina believed that good acting was more important than a great body or a knock-'em-dead smile. After all, if looks were all that mattered, she'd already be a star.

To some people, that would sound egotistical. But Christina had long ago accepted that she'd lucked out in the physical-attributes department. She had long, slim legs, fine straw-colored hair, naturally perfect teeth, and sparkling blue eyes that worked magic with camera lenses. She'd been a professional model since she was a little kid.

But now she wanted more.

Christina parked the VW in front of the Baxters' house. Randi started to get out, then hesitated.

"Are you sure you want to do this?" she asked, sounding worried.

"Do what?" Christina asked.

"Audition for this movie. I mean . . . like you might really get bummed out if you don't get a part."

Christina smiled. Randi always looked out for her. And she always looked out for Randi. They'd been friends since first grade.

"I'll be disappointed if I don't get something . . . even a walk-on will do. But if they turn me down, it won't kill me."

"You sure?"

Christina frowned. It was unlike Randi to be so cautious. She was the one who always encouraged her to go for it when a new challenge popped up.

"Sure, I'm sure. Acting is just the most important thing in my life . . ." She grinned to let her friend know that she was joking.

Randi studied her doubtfully. "Well, just remember . . . you already have a super modeling career. I'd chop off both my arms to pose for the cover of *Seventeen* like you did."

"That would make a pretty gross cover," Christina pointed out, giggling.

Randi laughed along with her. "You're too much. Want to come in for a few minutes? We can make sandwiches and study my notes for tomorrow's history exam."

"No thanks. I have to memorize the sides for my audition tomorrow."

"Sides?"

"The script pages Marsha faxed to me."

Randi smiled good-naturedly. "Okay. See you tomorrow in school."

Christina watched her very best friend in all the world disappear inside the front door of her family's modest wood-frame house. Randi was the best. She never gave up on Christina even though Chris was a lousy student and Randi herself was a semi-genius. If it hadn't been for her, Christina probably wouldn't have passed chemistry or calculus last year. It was the chubby, plain, but brainy president of the honor society who'd helped her with homework and coached her before every test when modeling assignments ate up nearly every minute of Christina's afternoons and weekends.

5

Randi never seemed to be hurt when Christina didn't have time to do fun things with her that other friends did together—like shop all Saturday at the mall or take off for a day at the beach. Most importantly, she never begrudged Christina her dreams.

Christina's first dream had appeared when she was seven years old. Her mother told her to look in the Sears catalogue and choose three things she'd like to have for Christmas. Slowly turning the pages of the "Wish Book," Christina solemnly studied every dress, doll, sparkly piece of play jewelry, and kiddy stereo system.

"Well?" her mother finally asked. "What will we put on Santa's list?"

"Her." Christina pointed.

"What?" Mrs. English frowned. Like her husband, she was a lawyer and tended to take things literally. "You mean the black velvet dress? It's very pretty, dear, but not your color—"

"No," Christina interrupted impatiently. "Not the dress. I want to be *her*. I want to be in the 'Wish Book.'"

Nothing her mother or father could say discouraged their daughter. For an entire year, Christina insisted that she wanted to be a model, although she didn't really understand what hard work and sacrifice that would require. As a last resort, Mr. English took his daughter to a professional photographer. The woman had done some legal work for him but also supplied fashion shots for the *Hartford Courant* Sunday magazine section. He made a pact with Christina. If the photographer said she didn't have what it took to be a child model, she would stop pestering her parents about it.

The woman took one look at the skinny little girl with wispy blonde hair and sunny smile—and pronounced her incredibly photogenic. That very day, she snapped Christina's first head shots—the 8-by-10 black-and-white glossy photos that she'd need to start her professional portfolio.

Christina worked like a slave, giving up all of her playtime to pose for catalogue photos and advertising supplements. Her parents rearranged their already busy schedules and took turns driving her to jobs. Dragging makeup kit, curling iron, spare shoes and underclothes, and old sheets to spread on dusty floors to protect clients' expensive clothing, they drove all over New England and New York. It was as much work for her mother and father as it was for Christina. But Christina's dream was realized. She made it into the "Wish Book."

But her career didn't stop there.

Two years ago, the photo editor of *Seventeen* chose her to appear on the magazine's July cover. No sooner did the issue hit the stands than her manager was besieged with calls from agents eager to book Christina for major advertisements in *Vogue* and *Cosmo,* as well as for TV commercials and cosmetic advertising campaigns. She'd even traveled with eight other teen models to do a shoot in London. It had been the most exciting week of her life.

Then, last summer, it suddenly hit her that she'd been modeling for nine years, and it felt like a lifetime. She had more than enough money saved up for college, and she supposed she should feel grateful that she'd been as successful as she had been. She wasn't satisfied, though. She wanted more . . . and it didn't seem wrong to dream one more dream.

"I want to try acting," she'd told Marsha, who also handled young actors.

"It's a whole new ball game . . . a cutthroat business," Marsha warned her. "You'll need an acting coach— probably several before you're ready—and experience in local productions."

"Whatever it takes, I'll do it," Christina declared.

She meant what she said. She used money she'd earn-ed modeling to pay for expensive acting lessons, for transportation to auditions, for voice and dancing classes. She landed a few small roles in amateur productions, a couple in school plays, and a position with a professional touring company last summer.

But her dream was to be on the big screen. To mingle with Hollywood stars and maybe . . . just maybe . . . someday be one of them.

Getting Theodore Dreising to notice her might be her big chance—if she didn't blow it.

The next day after school, Christina drove thirty miles south of her hometown, Hanover, Connecticut, to New Haven. Of course, it would have been nicer if Dreising weren't shooting a horror film, Christina thought as she walked down the hallway of the office building where the *Dark Memories* production company was auditioning.

But, she reminded herself, *a good actress can handle any role*.

Besides, Dreising was a powerful name in Hollywood. His movies attracted lots of attention. Actors lucky enough to earn parts with just one or two lines sometimes went on to do major films with other directors.

She looked up from the three pages of script she'd been glancing over. In front of her, a door was marked SUITE 305.

When she walked into the reception room, her heart fell. The place was jammed with a hundred or more actors, young and old men and women, all waiting to read for the handful of parts being auditioned by the casting director today.

"Chris!" a voice called out from the crowd.

She searched the sea of faces for a familiar one. At last she spotted a girl with massive hair and vivid makeup, who was jumping up and down like a crazed jack-in-the-box and waving excitedly.

Beryl Washington.

Glad to see someone she knew, Christina smiled and worked her way across the room. Unfortunately, another familiar face looked up at her from behind a newspaper.

"Hi, Mrs. Washington," Christina said politely.

"Hello, Christina dear," Mavis Washington replied coolly. Beryl's mother was dressed in a loud purple jacket and gold lamé pants that made her heavy legs look like elephant thighs. "Are they interviewing extras today, too?"

"I'm reading for a part," Christina said as calmly as she could manage. Since the first day she'd met Beryl Washington's mother, Christina had despised the woman. She thought her rude, spiteful, and pushy.

"Oh, really . . . That should be quite a challenge for you, dear."

"Mother, stop that!" Beryl groaned. She gave Christina a friendly smile. "Chris has done almost as much acting as I have."

Although Beryl might have intended her comment as a subtle dig, it was, in a way, true. As secretary of the Thespian Society at Hanover High, Beryl had accumulated quite a bit of experience in school productions. She'd played Anne in *The Diary of Anne Frank*, Alice in *The Glass Menagerie*, and one of the Trapp family daughters in *The Sound of Music*. However, she'd never done anything on a professional level. Her mother insisted on managing her, which was the kiss of death as far as Christina was concerned.

"I guess I should wish you to break a leg," Christina said, trying to be nice.

"Yeah," Beryl said with a nervous laugh. "Except, in a film like this, 'break a leg' sounds like a bad omen."

Christina nodded. "You've got that right."

She looked around the room. All of the chairs were taken, and there was barely space enough to stand without touching the people next to her. Two more hopefuls

9

opened the door, took a quick, disappointed look at the crowd, and left.

"Has anyone gone in yet?" Chris asked, staring at the door that must have led to the inner offices.

"A few," said Beryl. "They were out in less than a minute. Must not be what they're looking for."

Christina sighed. If she didn't pass the first test by simply looking right to the casting director—who'd undoubtedly been told exactly what Dreising wanted—she might not even get to read.

The office door opened, and a young man burst through. Angry tears glittering in his eyes, he stared straight ahead as he shoved his way through the crowd and out the door.

"Another one bites the dust," Beryl commented dryly.

Christina swallowed the lump in her throat, surprised at how desperately she wanted a part in this film. Her palms felt moist. She quickly dried them on her denim miniskirt.

The inner office door swung open again. A young woman carrying a clipboard stepped through.

She had short tan-colored hair and a mass of freckles across her nose and cheekbones. If she'd smiled even a little, she probably would have been pretty. But her mouth formed a rigid line across her face. Her eyes were as dull as old shoe leather as they scanned the room.

"Beryl Washington," she read off her list.

Beryl pushed Christina out of the way in her excitement. "That's me!" she called out.

"Wait!" Mavis cried, suddenly coming alive. Dropping her newspaper, she pulled a hairbrush out of her purse and aimed for Beryl's teased locks.

"Hurry up," the woman with the clipboard chided. "*He* is waiting."

From her tone, she might have been talking about the president of the United States . . . or God.

10

"Hold onto your hat!" Beryl snapped.

The young woman's eyes narrowed, then slipped toward Christina, as if guessing the two girls were together.

Christina smiled an apology for Beryl. "Nerves," she murmured.

Christina suspected that the clipboard lady was more than a receptionist. If she were Dreising's personal assistant, or the casting director herself, Beryl had just made a powerful enemy.

At last Mrs. Washington released her daughter with a final pat to her mane, and Beryl disappeared into the office.

As soon as they were gone, Mavis snatched up her copy of *Variety* and continued reading.

Christina didn't mind being snubbed. Taking advantage of a few minutes of quiet, she closed her eyes and whispered lines from the pages clutched in her hand.

Her stomach knotted. She could hardly think over the message her heart thudded in her chest: *This is your big chance . . . big chance . . . big chance. Don't blow it!*

Less than five minutes later, Beryl returned to the waiting room, her cheeks aglow.

"Momma! I did it!" she cried. People turned and stared at her, hungry for clues to what the casting director was looking for. "Just like you said—I really hammed it up, and Mr. Dreising said he was sure they'd call me."

"The director himself! He's here?" Mavis beamed at her daughter, then turned all business. "You didn't sign anything, did you?"

"No, Momma."

"Good girl." Mavis heaved herself to her feet and slung her huge purse over one shoulder. "Soon as the contract arrives, we get us a good lawyer."

"Christina English!" the clipboard lady called.

"That's me."

11

Christina stepped forward as Beryl and her mother departed jubilantly. Her mind whirled, trying to recall every piece of advice her most recent acting coach had drilled into her while preparing her for the audition.

Smile. Look the casting director straight in the eye. Let him know you're easy to work with. Be professional.

The woman led Christina into a room stripped of all furniture except for one long table with three folding chairs behind it and one in front. On the floor beside the table was a mountain of 8-by-10 glossies with the name, address, and resumé of an actor printed on the back of each one.

Panic seized Christina. Nevertheless, she forced herself to take a step toward the desk and fake a warm, confident smile.

The clipboard lady said, "I'm Amanda Perry, Mr. Dreising's personal assistant."

She gestured to the man and woman seated at the table. The man wore jeans and a black T-shirt under a wrinkled linen jacket. His long, ebony hair was pulled back into a ponytail. The woman was dressed in a stylish, navy-blue business suit.

"This is Theodore Dreising, director of *Dark Memories*," Ms. Perry introduced her boss. "On his right is Jacki Fielding, of Fielding and Associates, our casting director."

Everyone said a polite hello and shook Chris's hand.

Ms. Fielding said, "Your head shot, Chris?"

Christina handed her photo to Ms. Perry, who passed it to the casting director. It was called a head shot because it showed only from her shoulders up. Her blonde hair was brushed out smooth and uncurled, and it gleamed under the photographer's lights. She looked straight into the camera. Wearing very little makeup in this photo, she looked young, very innocent and vulnerable—which Marsha had said was perfect for a movie like Dreising's,

12

where most of the characters were going to be hunted down and slaughtered.

Ms. Fielding studied the photo without comment, then handed it to Dreising. The director looked at the photograph critically, glancing up several times to compare it with Christina who was seated in front of him.

She shifted her feet, feeling as if he were sizing her up for a coffin—which was where most of his actresses ended up in his films.

"So—" he said at last. "Christina . . . or is it Chris or Chrissy?"

"Chris is okay," she said.

"Chris, then. Are you prepared to read for us today?"

She coughed lightly to clear her throat. "Yes." Tucking her script pages into her purse, she stood up and delivered the few short lines Marsha had told her to memorize.

When she was finished, silence filled the room. Dreising looked speculatively at Ms. Fielding. The casting director tapped the eraser end of her pencil on the table and tipped her head to one side as if to say, *Not bad, but nothing special.*

"Of course, it's hard to tell much from just a couple of lines," Christina burst out. "I . . . I've prepared something else if you have time to hear it." She held her breath, her ears ringing, terrified that she'd been too bold.

Dreising frowned, his heavy black brows lowering.

"Perhaps another time," Jacki Fielding said.

"No—" Dreising cut her off. "What do you want to do for us?"

Christina ran her tongue between her lips. "Claire's monologue from *The Breakfast Club.*"

"Good film, good choice," Dreising commented, studying her over the tips of his fingers. "Go ahead."

Christina drew a long, slow breath to compose her hopscotching nerves and allowed herself to slip into

13

character. This was a scene in which a girl about her own age bared her soul to a taunting classmate, admitting a very personal truth . . . that she was a virgin.

Christina hoped she could pull off the warring emotions that had made the film a modern teen classic. She gave it her all, directing her lines straight at Dreising, lashing out at him as if he were her tormentor.

He watched her unblinkingly with eyes that seemed to darken with each word. When Christina at last finished, she felt physically exhausted and emotionally wiped out. She waited for him to comment.

He said nothing, only stared at her thoughtfully.

Her heart floundered like a delicate butterfly caught in a hurricane and slammed against a brick building. More than anything, she wanted to run from the room. Instead, she sat down again and returned Dreising's steely gaze, sure at least that she'd done her best. If he didn't recognize talent when he saw it—well, that was his problem. Her knees shook. She pressed her hands down on her kneecaps to stop them.

"Thank you very much for coming today," Jacki Fielding said politely. She nodded at Amanda Perry.

Dreising's assistant stood up and strode toward the door, as if expecting Christina to follow. While walking, she tossed questions over her shoulder.

"You live nearby?"

"In Hanover—ten minutes from Clayton State Park where you'll be shooting."

"Transportation?"

"I drive . . . my own car."

"Manager?"

"Marsha Sherman. Her number's on my resumé."

"Right." She held open the door for Christina. "We'll be in touch."

Sure you will, thought Christina grimly. A bitter taste filled her mouth as she imagined her photo discarded on the heap beside Dreising's table.

Chapter 2

Steve Jackson screamed his lungs out. Shoving his toes against the edge of the blue foam wrestling mat, he slid forward on his steel folding chair. He was in the middle of the row of his Hanover High teammates. On the far side of the gymnasium was a second line of chairs, occupied by the Bridgewater team, also wearing fitted one-piece singlets. The bleachers above the wrestlers overflowed with students.

"Pin him! Pin him!" Steve shouted, his clenched fists pounding into his knees.

The crowd exploded into cheers as the home-team wrestler slipped his opponent's grip, executing a clever escape. One point for Hanover. But the match wasn't over.

"Come *on*, Bobby, get hold of his arm . . . watch out for his leg! Hold him!"

But no amount of coaching from the sidelines could help Steve's teammate. The Bridgewater wrestler crooked a muscled leg up and around Bobby, flipping him onto his back. Within five seconds, he'd forced both of the other boy's shoulder blades into the mat. The ref blew his whistle, signaling a pin for the visiting team.

Steve groaned, rubbing the heels of his hands, already damp with sweat, into his eye sockets. Bobby had trained

15

hard and remembered Coach's tactical advice, but he didn't have the killer instinct necessary to be a top wrestler. Steve, on the other hand, had been state champ in the 145-pound weight class for two years. The guys on the team called him the Doomsday Machine. Doomsday for short.

He pushed himself onto his feet as his team rose to huddle. It was his turn on the mat. The coach mumbled a few words of strategy, then slapped him on the butt for luck.

"Go!" the team shouted, breaking huddle.

Steve won the toss and chose to start in the down position—on his hands and knees. His opponent bent over him with one arm wrapped around Steve's middle, the other hand braced on his arm. Being on the bottom was usually considered the weaker starting position, but Steve had learned to use it to his advantage. If he did everything right, within five to ten seconds he'd escape the hold and earn his first point.

The ref's whistle shrieked. Steve skillfully slipped the Bridgewater wrestler's grip and vaulted to his feet.

The kid looked shocked . . . then worried.

"Shoot! Shoot! Shoot!" the home crowd chanted.

Gritting his teeth on his mouth guard, Steve glared at the other boy, who was sweating a river. They circled each other in low crouches. Steve picked his moment and method of attack.

Lunging forward, he wrapped his arms around the boy's left knee and pulled it up toward his own chest. Steve drove forward with his hips and lifted his opponent clear of the mat before taking him down with a thud.

"Pin! Pin! Pin!" chanted the crazed Hanover fans.

Steve adjusted his hold on the squirming Bridgewater wrestler. The boy was strong and smart, twisting his body around to try for a reverse. But Steve knew all the tricks. He replaced his hold, captured the boy's free arm, and twisted it sharply while flipping him onto his back.

16

After a few seconds of intense pressure, driving the kid's shoulder blades into the mat, Steve made his pin.

The crowd went wild.

The ref raised Steve's arm above his head to signal that he was the winner of the match. Without really thinking about what he was doing, Steve glanced around the bleachers. Rows of familiar faces beamed back at him, shouting their approval. But the only one who counted wasn't there. He didn't know why he always looked for her. She never came.

When the meet was over, the Hampton wrestlers retreated victoriously to their locker room. Everyone was high, even Coach.

"Remember, guys, we stay in training. No booze, no smoking. Tough workouts every day. Let's be in top form for regionals next week."

A roar filled the locker room, and when the sounds of celebration finally ceased echoing off the cinder-block walls and everyone quit smacking each other with towels and squirting soda from bottles, Steve took his shower. He washed up slowly, sudsing his hair a second time, rinsing longer than necessary. He wanted to give the others time to leave so he could be alone for a while.

At last, they left—Bobby, Chuck, Ralph, Clay, Wes, Coach, and the rest. He could hear people outside the locker room congratulating them. Parents and friends, girls . . . lots of girls. Wrestling groupies always hung around outside the locker room. Any of the girls would have been thrilled to accompany him to Flannigan's for nachos and sodas after the meet. But Steve wasn't interested.

With a sigh, he glanced around the empty room, then padded barefoot across the cement floor to his locker at the very back corner and worked the combination. He pulled out his sports bag, and out of that his clean clothes, and dressed. Tucking his sweaty singlet into the separate plastic-lined section of his bag, he reached down to the bottom for his comb.

His fingers brushed against something crisp. Then he remembered.

Slowly he withdrew the page he'd torn out of a newspaper several months ago. Steve studied the sweetly smiling face of the girl in the photo. Underneath, a caption read: *Christina English, Hanover High student, to appear in West Haven Theater production of "The Crucible."*

He studied her sparkling eyes. The black-and-white photo didn't do them justice. China-blue they were. And her pale-blonde hair always looked as light and clean as sunshine. She was the most beautiful girl he'd ever met, and nice too. Not at all snobby like you might expect of a model and actress. Most kids her age would get an attitude.

But not Chris. She was . . . she was *perfect*.

Carefully Steve tore a piece of clear tape from the roll he kept in his locker for just such moments. He found an empty spot inside his locker among all the other clippings from newspapers and fashion magazines, then added this newest picture of Christina to his collection. He'd also snapped several photographs of her with his brother's 35-mm camera. Two following school plays at the cast parties, one as she was leaving her house one morning, another of her wearing sunglasses and sitting behind the wheel of her VW. Of course she hadn't known he was taking the pictures. He'd been very careful not to let her or anyone else see him.

Standing back, he studied her many different moods and poses. It struck him that anyone seeing the inside of his locker would say he was obsessed. But he didn't think he was. He just liked her . . . a lot.

Savoring one last look at his secret gallery, Steve closed the locker and clamped shut the combination lock.

Chapter 3

The day following Christina's trip to New Haven, Marsha Sherman telephoned.

"The casting director wants you to come back for a second reading," she announced, excitement tingeing her voice.

"You're kidding!"

"Nope. This is for real, kiddo. Get your tail down to New Haven straight after school today." Chris could hear Marsha munching on something while she talked. The woman seemed to never take time off from work to eat.

"That probably means I'm being considered for a part with a couple of lines. Super!"

However, after her return audition that afternoon, Amanda Perry took her aside and started asking a string of strange questions.

"What do you think of Kurt Richmond?"

"He's okay, I guess."

"Do you have a boyfriend, Chris?"

"I—well, no."

And, most peculiar of all: "How would you feel about working closely with Kurt for long periods of time?"

Then Christina *knew*.

Oh, wow! I'm being considered for a major role!

Suddenly she felt both jubilant and sick to her stomach

at the same time. Everything was happening much faster than she'd expected. There followed a couple of days when she chickened out every other hour and called Marsha, begging her to withdraw her name.

She'd imagined slowly working her way into films the way she'd done with modeling. Getting a lead role would take a lot of hard work, she reasoned. But, for reasons no one could explain to her, she was being handed the world on a silver platter, and she didn't quite trust her incredibly good luck.

A *Dreising* film! Her first time out! The thought of it sent shivers up her spine, not all of them pleasurable.

"Just be grateful and say yes," Marsha advised. "The contract terms look great, and you'll do just fine. You have a lot of talent, Chris. Chances like this don't come along often."

Christina swallowed her fears and signed on the dotted line. For some reason, she felt as if she were signing her life away.

The next day in school, no one got a thing done. The junior and senior classes were too busy gossiping. Sophomores didn't have enough upper-class contacts to know what was going on, so they spent the day trying to figure out what all the excitement was about. And freshmen wandered the corridors in their usual confused daze, afraid to ask what was up because they still were intimidated by upperclassmen.

Word had gotten out that four Thespian Club members were going to miss several weeks of school because they had jobs in a movie that was being shot nearby. Jennifer Adkins and Beryl Washington had landed parts as extras, but might get to speak one or two lines. John Washington, Beryl's older brother, was a production assistant, which meant he'd be running errands for the director and his crew. That didn't sound terribly glamorous to some until they realized that he'd get paid twice as much as anyone who worked bagging groceries or clerking at the video store. Plus, he'd be smack in the middle of a hot movie in the making, which was a massive kick!

Then there was Christina English. She had been cast to play the lead opposite Kurt Richmond!

All day long, kids who'd never spoken to Christina sought her out to congratulate her. She was thrilled to have so much attention, but a little worried too.

"I want to have friends," she admitted to Randi over lunch that day. "I mean, I hardly have time for even one friend—you—because of the modeling. I really miss having a social life."

"You mean dating?" Randi asked knowingly.

Christina lifted one shoulder and smiled shyly as she pulled her apple, cup of yogurt, and juice box out of a brown paper sack and arranged them on the cafeteria table. Pizza with fries was the special today, and the dining area smelled of oregano, tomatoes, and cheese. But Christina had learned long ago that cafeteria food was murder on a model's figure.

"Yeah, I guess dating. It's just always been so hard to make friends and have time for fun things. You know how it is. I leave straight from school every afternoon for a lesson or a job. I have to squeeze in homework sometime. And Marsha always books me up for weekends."

"What a tough life!" Randi rolled her eyes dramatically. "Flying to Florida to pose in bathing suits, then zipping off to Colorado to pretend-ski in a cute little snowsuit."

Christina laughed and elbowed her friend in the ribs. "Knock it off. I'm serious. I may have exciting memories, but they don't include guys."

"What about guy models?" Randi asked curiously, lowering her voice. "All those nights away from home in exotic places?"

"You'd be the first one to know if there was ever anyone serious." Christina hesitated, then shrugged. "Besides, it's not a good idea to mix romance with business. I don't date other models or actors."

"I would," Randi stated emphatically. "What are you waiting for, anyway?"

Christina groaned in frustration. "I don't know what I want. I guess, sometimes, I'd just like to be normal. You know—call friends on the phone and chat for hours, throw a party or go to one, spend a whole Saturday tanning on a beach."

"Maybe you can't have both," Randi suggested sensibly. "A lot of girls would kill to be you."

"Maybe you're right," Christina murmured. She sipped her drink thoughtfully.

After another minute, Randi said, "You did go steady with a couple of guys."

"For a short time in middle school . . . then last year."

"Kevin Smith in eighth grade," Randi remembered.

"And John Washington my junior year."

Randi's eyes twinkled. "John seems so nice. Much nicer than his sister." She scrunched up her nose in distaste.

"Oh, Beryl's not so bad. She just tries too hard sometimes. And I think that having a mother like hers must be rough."

"The woman's a human bulldozer," Randi muttered. "I've never seen anyone so pushy."

Christina took a bite of her apple. In some ways she wished her own parents took more of an interest in her career. These days, Regina and Robert English were so busy with their law practices that they rarely had time to attend auditions with Christina. Since she'd started driving, that was no longer a necessity.

However, they did seem genuinely pleased whenever Christina did well. One or the other of them attended at least one performance of every play she'd been in. When the contract for the film arrived, her mom had spent two nights studying it, word by word, before she let Christina sign. So they did care, she reminded herself. They just seemed to be heading in different directions these days.

Maybe, thought Christina, a little sadly, *that's part of growing up*.

"What went wrong with John?" Randi asked.

Christina's thoughts snapped back to her conversation with Randi. She smiled vaguely. "Oh . . . I don't know. We were just so different."

"Like he's a jock?"

"He's a really good guy," Christina said fondly. "But he's so deep into sports—pitching for varsity baseball, Babe Ruth league all summer, then basketball and indoor track. I couldn't swing a bat within a mile of a ball or run a hundred yards if my life depended on it. I never had time to play games outside like other kids. I guess I just feel hopelessly klutzy around a boy who's massively physical." She sighed. "I don't think I could ever fall for a jock again."

"Well," Randi said, munching on corn chips out of a bag, "there are a lot of other kinds of guys who'd give ten years of their lives to date a cover girl."

Christina took a vicious bite of her apple and tossed the core into her lunch bag.

"That's just it," she muttered in exasperation. "I don't want to be anyone's trophy. I just want some boy to like me because we have fun doing things together and . . . and maybe there will even be a few sparks when we kiss."

"You expect him to overlook all that gorgeousness?" Randi teased.

Christina cast Randi a dirty look. "Give me a break, will you?"

Steve Jackson looked up from his three-inch-thick roast-beef sandwich, watching Christina and her friend

23

walk out of the cafeteria. Sitting at the table beside theirs, he'd overheard the last part of their conversation. His heart felt like a lump of lead in his chest.

She hates jocks, he thought miserably.

It didn't seem fair that he'd almost worked up enough courage to call her again. Three months ago he'd asked her out, but she'd given him some story about having to work. After that, he'd been afraid to ask again for fear she'd turn him down. Next time the excuse might not be as gentle on his ego.

He shut his eyes for a moment, regretting that he'd never have the chance to get to know her better. Of course, just as importantly, she'd never learn what he was all about. He was more than just a jock—a lot more. He was sure he could make her happy. *But she isn't going to give me a chance*, he thought bitterly.

It just didn't seem fair.

Christina stood outside a trailer marked AMANDA PERRY/ASSISTANT TO THE DIRECTOR. Along with fifteen others, it had been towed to the middle of the woods in Clayton State Park. Formerly a private estate, the park was a popular tourist attraction overlooking the Connecticut River. The huge stone castle had been built to resemble a much larger castle in Germany. Along with its ornate gardens and the surrounding woods, it was to be the location for *Dark Memories*. By now the production company had closed the area off to the public and begun setting up.

The long gray trailers, lined up alongside each other, were used as offices and dressing rooms. Generators, lights, cameras, and assorted vehicles stood ready. About a half mile below the castle, the parking area had been enlarged and reserved for crew and cast. A manned security shack stood at the bottom of the hill, to discourage curious passersby or aggressive fans. Everything seemed ready for moviemaking.

To the right of Amanda Perry's door, someone had taped a cardboard sign that read ALL TALENT REPORT HERE.

Nerve butterflies fluttered in Christina's stomach. Last night she'd been so excited she hadn't been able to sleep. She slowly raised her hand and knocked on the trailer door.

"It's open!" a voice called from inside.

Climbing two wooden stairs, Christina stepped inside. Amanda perched on the front edge of a small metal desk, studying Christina as she blinked, adjusting to the dim light.

"Hi!" Christina said brightly to cover her nervousness. "Guess I'm supposed to report to you?"

"Right." Amanda didn't crack a smile.

She appeared to be about ten years older than Christina. Her short hair clung to the contours of her head. She wore no makeup to emphasize her nice, high cheekbones or pretty almond-shaped eyes.

Looking at her from a model's perspective Christina thought, *With a little effort she could be spectacular.*

"Sit down." Amanda directed, busily flipping through papers on her clipboard. "You need to fill out a bunch of forms." She waved her toward a leather armchair.

Christina took a step forward, then jerked to a halt. Startled, she sucked in her breath. A boy was slumped casually into the curve of the chair's cushions. She had thought she and Amanda were alone.

On first glance, he might have been any high school senior, hanging out, waiting for an odd job. But she recognized him immediately. He wasn't just anyone.

When he looked up at her, his deep-blue eyes twinkled with interest. He kicked back his head, and a wave of blond hair lifted off his forehead for a second before falling back over one eye—the same way it did on a thousand theater screens across the country.

25

"Hi," he said, with a hint of California cool. "I hear we'll be working together."

Christina swallowed, then swallowed again, unable to speak. She stuck out her hand to shake his. "You're . . . um . . . you're Kurt Richmond," she finally managed.

"Yup." He grinned, as if pleased his mere presence had rattled her.

"This is Christina English." Amanda introduced her to Kurt, watching both of them warily. "Your leading lady."

"Smooth," Kurt pronounced, letting his eyes drift down to the toes of Christina's tennis shoes then all the way up her long blue-jeaned legs to her wide, blue eyes. "Okay if I call you Chris?"

"S-s-sure."

"Well, Chris," he said, sitting up a little straighter in the chair, "I think we'll have a lot of fun doing this movie. Ted's a real blast."

Ted, she translated for herself, *Theodore Dreising*. She wondered if she would ever dare call their director by his first name.

"I have a great idea," Kurt suggested, giving her a playful wink. "How about you come over to my trailer, and we'll go over a few of our early scenes together? Sort of get a jump on things."

"Mind your manners, Kurt!" Amanda snapped. "Miss English is a local girl. This is her first film."

"That so? A virgin, huh?"

Christina hesitated a beat too long. "Oh—yeah." She laughed and went on quickly. "My first movie. But I've had a lot of stage experience and I've modeled since I was a little kid."

Amanda shoved a stack of papers and a pen into her hands. "Sign everywhere I've put a red check. These are standard information and release forms. The top one is your medical emergency card . . . in case there's an

26

accident on the set and we have to get hold of your parents or doctor."

Kurt rose from his seat and offered it to Christina. Sitting down with a smile of thanks, she bent over the first sheet. Kurt perched on the arm of her chair. He watched silently as she wrote her address and phone number.

"This is pretty country around here," he commented. "Lots of green hills, trees, and quiet. Not at all like I pictured the East Coast."

She went on writing.

"I'm thinking about buying a house out this way."

Christina looked up. "A house?" Kids her age didn't usually talk about investing in real estate. She reminded herself that Kurt could probably afford a dozen houses.

"Yeah. I'd like a place within limo distance of New York City. I've thought about doing something on Broadway."

"Really?"

"Sure. If the right play . . . the right part came along. I think an actor should experience as many different types of roles as possible."

"Kurt," Amanda interrupted, "how about running along to wardrobe? You were due there half an hour ago."

The young actor's eyes darkened, and a muscle at the side of his neck twitched. Christina remembered what she'd heard about Kurt's temper. She held her breath as the star and Dreising's assistant locked glares.

Slowly, the tension around Kurt's eyes smoothed away. He glanced back at Christina, smiling easily, the anger apparently gone. "Watch out for Amanda. She likes to stick her nose into everyone's business," he warned, as if the woman wasn't in the room. "Even listens in on phone calls and reads other people's mail to make sure they're totally loyal to her master."

"Enough, Kurt!" Amanda growled.

"Gotta run, ladies," he chirped. Before Christina realized what he was about to do, he'd bent and dropped

27

a quick kiss on her cheek. "Come find me when you finish here, Chris. We really should get to know each other before filming starts. We'll be doing a couple of love scenes, ya know."

When Christina left Amanda's trailer twenty minutes later, she still felt flushed and confused by Kurt's lightning attempt at flirting with her. Despite his macho charm, she knew she had to concentrate on business.

She spent the rest of the morning getting to know the crew. Everyone had a specific behind-the-scenes job which seemed as important as any actor's role.

First she met the wardrobe lady and her assistants, then the makeup artists and special-effects coordinator. There was also a stunt coordinator and her talented team, the director of photography, and the lighting and camera crews with dozens of workers with unfamiliar titles like gaffer and grip.

Christina was leaving wardrobe for the second time that day when she spotted a familiar face.

"John!" she cried happily.

"Hey, I was hoping I'd run into you," he called out, grinning as he jogged across the grass toward her. He was tall and lanky, built like a basketball player even though his favorite sport was baseball. "How's life as a star?"

"So far, just a lot of paperwork and trying to remember people's names. I can memorize pages of dialogue, but I've got a lousy memory for names. How's your job?"

He shrugged. "Dreising keeps me busy. Nothing very important, but the money's great. I can really use it for my college fund."

"Are you still planning on going to U Conn?" Christina asked. The University of Connecticut's main campus was located in Storrs, only twenty-five miles from where they were today.

"Definitely—if I can scrape the cash together. My

mom works hard, but she can't support the two of us and save up tuition money."

"It must be hard on her, being alone," Christina said sympathetically.

When she'd dated John, she'd gotten to know his family pretty well. John was the man of the household. His father had left the family when both children were very young. Christina and Beryl had become friendly, although not as close as she and Randi had always been. Christina sensed that Beryl was jealous of her success. Mrs. Washington was pleasant only to those people who might further her daughter's acting career. Nevertheless, Christina and John had stayed friends after they'd broken up.

"Yeah, well, Mom does the best she can," John remarked solemnly.

"Can't you get a scholarship?" Christina asked.

"Not really. My grades aren't all that hot. As long as I'm working and playing varsity sports, I don't have much time for homework."

Christina nodded. She sure knew what a struggle balancing school and a job could be. "Is Beryl around?" she asked.

John's glance jumped to the other side of the set, as if something had caught his eye. "Beryl?" he repeated. "Naw. Extras don't have to report until tomorrow."

"Too bad. I thought the three of us might have lunch together."

"Yeah, well . . ." He seemed distracted, in a rush to leave all of a sudden. "Maybe tomorrow. Listen, my boss is waving for me . . . I gotta go. See ya round."

"Sure," she said. "See ya."

Frowning, she watched John leave. She was concerned about him. He worked so hard, worried so much about his mother and sister.

She was heading for makeup, lost in her thoughts, when someone grasped her shoulder. Spinning around, she found herself facing Theodore Dreising.

He wore dusty Levi's, a blue T-shirt with a Mets decal over a modest beer belly, and a Baltimore Orioles cap on his head. Black, bushy eyebrows hovered like storm clouds over dark eyes. His thick hair was pulled back with a plain rubber band. He wasn't much taller than she was, but his hand on her shoulder seemed large and heavy.

"You finding your way around okay?" he asked.

"Yes, sir," she answered nervously as he at last moved his hand away. "I was just on my way to makeup."

He grimaced. "Maybe that's not such a good idea."

"Huh?"

"I want my still photographer to take a few shots of you before the makeup man starts gooping you up. You know—before-and-after pics."

"Will there be that much difference?" she asked.

He let out a low, rolling laugh. "You won't recognize yourself, sweetheart. You've read the script, haven't you?"

"Yes. Three times."

"Tell me the story."

Christina chewed her lower lip, puzzled. After all, he must know the script forward and backward.

"I want to be sure you've grasped the true essence of the tale," he explained. "You must understand your role in the story to play it well."

Christina nodded. There didn't seem much to understand in the typical slasher film, but she might as well humor him.

"Let's see now," she began. "It starts almost a hundred years ago with Sir Neville Griswold, the owner of the castle."

"Right. In 1895 to be exact. Go on."

"Well, he was a famous stage actor, very talented, but his ego kind of sent him off the deep end. He boasted that he could deceive anyone—even Death itself."

"Yes!" Dreising's eyes glowed with excitement. "He was perhaps the first FX man, braving the ultimate challenge."

"Anyway," she continued, "years later, when his career started to fade, he married a beautiful young actress and brought her to his estate. They were happy for a short time. But while she became more and more successful, he began to have trouble getting roles, and he became insanely jealous. He imagined that she was cheating on him with her current leading man. Although she was innocent, he murdered her."

"How?" Dreising demanded, his eyes glinting darkly.

Christina swallowed. Something about his enthusiasm for such a morbid subject bothered her, setting off little warning chimes inside her head.

"He . . . he stabbed her through the heart with a pearl-handled letter opener, a gift from her costar."

"And then what?"

"The police tracked him down in the castle gardens. When they cornered him, he swore they would never take him. His body would die by his own hand, but his spirit would live on after death and guard his beloved property—never again allowing a woman to be its mistress."

"Wonderful! Wonderful!" Dreising cried. He bounced on the balls of his feet like an overgrown toddler. "Then time jumps forward by a hundred years to the present and . . ." He gestured for her to go on with the story.

Christina cleared her throat, trying to ignore his antics. "Kurt and I show up at the castle, which has been converted to a ritzy bed-and-breakfast resort. Kurt plays a young medical student, and I'm his bride."

"And how are the two times linked?" Dreising asked.

"Sir Neville is a walking corpse . . . a zombie. He believes that every young woman who resembles his dead wife has come to steal his property. The second night of our honeymoon, Neville . . . he murders me."

she murmured, her voice fading away with the last words. They left her bones cold, her lip quivering.

"Precisely. He kills you the same way he killed his wife—a blade to the heart. But the young med student is so distraught by his darling's death, he digs up her body." Dreising took over the job of telling the gory tale. "Then he injects it with a chemical he and his medical friends have been experimenting with, which he believes will preserve the body until science discovers a way to heal her."

"But there's a problem," Christina pointed out. "He doesn't really know what he's doing, and the chemical brings his wife—me—temporarily back to life."

"Correct. Only now, you have no soul," Dreising stated dramatically. "Kurt realizes his mistake, but he can't bring himself to kill you . . . again."

"He's cheated Death," Christina whispered tightly. Her mouth felt dry, her palms sticky with sweat.

Dreising seemed lost in a daze, his eyes foggy, fixed on some distant place far beyond the spot where they stood in the clearing between trailers and among tangles of electrical cable.

"A crime against nature," he breathed. "The most horrid of all." He abruptly faced her, his dark eyes boring into her. "The young man realizes there is only one solution to the tragedy. He returns his zombie wife to the castle where Sir Neville claims her as his bride. They will live in their shadowy half-life together, forever haunting the castle grounds."

Christina swallowed. "I guess the makeup will make me look really . . . dead?"

"If Gus does his job right," Dreising said with a gruesome smile.

"Oh." She self-consciously touched her cheek.

"Don't worry, it's only temporary." He looked at her hard. "You aren't having second thoughts about the part, are you?"

32

"No," she fibbed. "It should be interesting."

"Good girl." He patted her on the back with his big paw. "Come along then."

Dreising turned and started walking among light tripods and camera equipment. Christina followed.

"Have you seen your dressing room yet?" he asked. Within seconds, his voice had lost its almost hysterical excitement.

"No. I didn't realize I'd have a dressing room all to myself."

"Sure, you're my leading lady! Since we're here we might as well take a look and see if you have everything you'll need." He veered to the right and cut between two other trailers.

Her dressing room was compact, with white siding. It was parked beside a larger silver trailer marked with Kurt's name and a huge star. CHRISTINA ENGLISH was stenciled over her door. She didn't merit a star.

They went inside. The single room was furnished with a simple white dressing table, lighted mirror, and a narrow cot buried under a frilly white eyelet bedspread and a pile of fluffy pillows. The place was cramped, but cozy and reassuring.

"This is great!" Christina said, grinning. The chill of Dreising's horrible tale filtered from her bones as she gazed around the cheery dressing room.

"If you need anything, pick up the phone and call Amanda," he suggested. "She'll send someone with ice, soda, a pizza . . . anything." Dreising turned to face her, his eyes studying her intensely. "Any questions so far?"

"I can't think of any . . . but . . ." Christina hesitated. She had contemplated telling Dreising her reservations about doing a horror movie. It seemed the honest thing to do. And yet—

"What?" he asked impatiently.

"I . . . I sort of have a confession," she began timidly.

"Oh?"

"I, um, I hate horror flicks."

Observing his suddenly grim expression, she wondered if she'd made a serious mistake.

She hurried on, "Not just *your* films, of course. In fact, until this spring I wouldn't go to see any of them because I . . . well, they make my stomach churn. All that blood and gore . . ."

Dreising stared at her in disbelief. Then, to her surprise, he burst into thunderous laughter, rocking his head back so far his baseball cap fell off.

"I'm sorry, Mr. Dreising," Christina quickly apologized. "I really think you're a super director. I mean, you must be—everyone says you are! But I can't help—" She groaned and threw up her hands helplessly.

Dreising choked on a final chuckle. "Don't apologize. None of my producers can stand my movies either." He took a deep breath and wiped tears from the corners of his eyes. "But they're smart people. They know what makes money these days. On the other hand, I couldn't care less about money."

"You couldn't?" she asked.

"What I love is the challenge of making the impossible happen." He leaned over to pick up his cap. "Sure, we all know that dead people don't get up and walk around, no human being has ever really turned into a wolf under a full moon, demons don't live in sewers, and evil spirits rarely take over the bodies of children—with the possible exception of a few spoiled-brat stars I've known. But I started out in special effects—an FX man. I live for fooling people. Fake bullets, fake blood, fake death. It's almost as if I'm—"

"Playing God?" Christina murmured.

His eyes sparkled, and for a long moment he stared at her in the silence of the little trailer. "Exactly!" he whispered. "How many men get to make people live or die at their whim?"

Now, as before, his warped enthusiasm chilled her.

She bit down on her lip and stared at him. She wasn't aware that the door behind her had opened.

"Ms. English!" a sharp voice snapped.

Christina whipped around to find Amanda Perry glaring at her, arms crossed over her chest.

"You're late for makeup," Amanda informed her.

"Go easy on her, Mandy," Dreising said, adjusting his hat on his head so that the ponytail stuck out the back vent. "I held her up for stills. Let me go see when Jeff will be ready for her." He walked out of the trailer, shaking his head and chuckling to himself. "Doesn't like horror flicks . . ."

Christina and Dreising's assistant stood watching the door he'd passed through.

"He's a really strange man," Christina said at last.

"He is a *genius*," stated Amanda with surprising fervor.

Christina turned to study the woman, surprised by the emotion in her voice.

"Did you see *Red Flames*?" Amanda asked.

"No."

"You should. Ted developed a technique for making a person grow into a monster right before the audience's eyes. He combined time-lapse photography and animation using a computer. It was brilliant. After *Red Flames*, he could write his own ticket as an FX man."

"Instead, he started directing?" Christina guessed.

"Right. He turned his back on his profession to take on a new challenge. Everyone in the business said he was biting off more than he could chew. But he proved them wrong. His directing was brilliant!"

Amanda's eyes shone with an adoring light. Christina thought to herself: *I don't believe it. She's in love with him!* No wonder she stuck her nose into everyone's business, as Kurt had accused. She was protecting Dreising.

Amanda suddenly seemed to notice that she was being

analyzed. She blinked and straightened up, all business again.

"Don't think because he was palling around with you today he's always like that," Amanda informed her. "Ted's a perfectionist. If you don't work hard enough for him, he'll get rid of you faster than a hummingbird can blink. And one other thing—" She pointed a warning finger.

"Yes?" Christina asked.

"Don't even *think* of starting up with Kurt romantically. You can't take anything that boy says seriously. He comes on to all of his leading ladies. If you fall in love with him, you won't be able to concentrate on acting."

"I'll remember that," Christina promised.

They hadn't started shooting that week, but by the end of each day Christina was exhausted. When she wasn't trying to memorize her lines, she was being dragged from makeup to wardrobe to her line coach.

She saw Beryl only once. Her classmate was with a group of extras, being briefed by Amanda. Christina wondered if they were getting Amanda's shape-up-or-ship-out speech.

One night when Christina got home, she poured herself a glass of cold milk, grabbed a fistful of Oreos from the cookie jar, and trudged upstairs to her room. Flopping on her bed, she relaxed and munched. Dinner wouldn't be for another hour, she'd have time to digest a snack. She closed her eyes and daydreamed.

Lazily, she reached out to her answering machine. She hit the "play" button. The machine squealed as it rewound. After a click and a whir, it began replaying the first message.

"Hi, Chris! It's Randi. Just wanted to see how things are going in the fast lane. School is pretty boring without you. Call me when you get in."

Christina grinned. She missed having lunch and sharing a couple of classes every day with Randi. But she had to admit, she didn't miss school itself very much. Her teachers had given her assignments, which she still had to complete and drop off at the guidance office each Friday for as long as the movie was in production.

After a beep, the next message played.

"Chrissy, hon, this is Marsha. *Cosmo* called to offer you a yummy job for a fashion layout in their Christmas issue. Too bad you won't finish filming in time. But they were tremendously impressed when I told them you were starring in a Ted Dreising film. My guess is they'll call again and offer more money."

Christina giggled. Good old Marsha. She always saw the sweet side of a deal, even if on the surface it went sour.

Message three.

"Chris? Mom here. I'll be staying late at work, and Dad has a meeting in Hartford tonight. Grab yourself something from the freezer for dinner. See you later, doll!"

"Good grief," she groaned. "Frozen TV dinner again!"

Message four.

A deep voice, muffled as if speaking through a dense fog, reached out for her from the machine. "Chris-s-s-s-y baby, I been watchin' you. You're so-o-o-o pretty." The sinister voice snickered. "I hope you do good on this film, sweetheart, 'cause if you disappoint me . . . something terrible might happen. I'll be keeping an eye on your performance. Just think of me as your greatest fan!"

Chapter 4

Christina lay on her bed, her eyes locked on the ceiling, her body paralyzed with horror.

That voice! It had sounded familiar somehow. Yet she couldn't quite identify it because it had been distorted, as if the caller had spoken through layers of tissue paper or a towel.

For several minutes she couldn't move, couldn't think of what to do. The answering machine automatically rewound itself and clicked off. She could hear her heart thudding in her chest, sense her blood pumping furiously through her veins. Her mouth tasted like old sneakers. The walls closed in around her.

"Oh, God," she murmured shakily. *What am I going to do!*

At last Christina rolled onto her stomach and reached for her telephone. She punched in her mother's office number and let it ring a dozen times before hanging up.

Her father! No—he was in Hartford. She had no way of contacting him. Her hand shaking violently, Christina hit another seven digits.

"Baxter residence."

"Randi!" Christina gasped. "Get over here!"

"Is that you, Chris? You sound funny. You all right?"

"No, I—I'm not," she stammered. Somewhere in the house a floorboard creaked, and she was instantly alert, listening. But she heard no footsteps. "Please, don't ask questions," she hissed into the receiver. "Just come over."

"What's wrong?"

"I'll tell you when you get here." She hung up.

Running downstairs, Christina checked the doors on the first floor, then the wide glass slider in the basement that opened into the backyard. They were all locked. She went to the bay window in the living room that overlooked the driveway. Gripping the sill, she waited tensely for Randi's beat-up van to appear. It took nine minutes from the time Christina hung up the phone until Randi arrived, out of breath, on her doorstep.

"What took you so long?" Christina demanded, letting her in then bolting the door behind her.

"I had to get dressed. I was studying in my nightsnirt. What's the big deal?"

Christina grabbed her by the hand and headed for the stairs. "Come up to my room. There's something I want you to hear."

Pulling free, Randi braced her hands on her wide hips and glared skeptically at her. "You brought me all the way over here to listen to you practice your lines?"

"No! This is serious!" Christina insisted. "Someone left a message on my machine. It's scary as hell."

"You mean—like an obscene phone call?"

"Not exactly."

Christina considered the possibility. *Obscene phone call.* Put that way, the message sounded almost ordinary. Lots of people got obscene phone calls. For the first time she questioned her panicky reaction.

"You listen to it and tell me what you think."

Randi sat on Christina's bed while Christina replayed the part of the tape with the stranger's message. With every raspy word, Randi's eyes grew wider.

39

"Gee," she breathed at the end. "That's pretty creepy."

"I thought he sounded familiar," Christina said. "Does he remind you of anyone?"

"Are you sure it's a guy?"

"Well, the voice is pretty low."

"Could be a woman disguising her voice," Randi pointed out.

"You're right," Christina decided.

She vigorously rubbed her nose, an old habit that revisited her whenever she was thinking hard. It drove photographers crazy as her wandering fingers wiped away the bronze-toned makeup that made her look tan year-round, leaving a pale streak down her nose.

"What do you think I should do?" Christina asked at last.

Randi screwed up her face. "I don't know. It's probably just a prank. Some jerk who gets his kicks calling people he reads about in the newspaper. Your number is in the phone book, isn't it?"

"Yeah. But what kind of person gets turned on by scaring strangers?"

"A sicko." Randi patted Christina on the shoulder comfortingly. "Hey, if you ever read a newspaper, you'd know. This sort of thing happens all the time to celebrities."

"But it's never happened to *me* before," Christina insisted.

"If you're really bummed out, call the police," Randi suggested calmly.

"The police?" Christina scowled at her telephone. "Don't you think that's a little drastic?"

"So—just ignore the idiot. You'll probably never hear from him, or her, again. Got any cookies around?"

Christina let out a long breath, feeling much better now that Randi had dismissed the call as nonsense. "In the kitchen. Bet I can eat more than you."

"Wrong!" Randi cried, bolting for the stairs.

40

At last the filming began. Since the weather was mild and dry, Dreising began with outdoor scenes. Only later would his director of photography take advantage of the dark woods, maze-like gardens surrounding the castle, and the gloomy rooms inside.

Christina didn't look forward to shooting those scenes. She would die in one, then be brought back to half-life as a gruesome zombie.

However, today promised to be fun, and she was determined not to let one lousy phone call spoil it for her.

If I'm going to be in this business, she told herself firmly, *I'll have to get used to crank calls and nutty fans*.

First they shot a scene in which she and Kurt drove up the road to the romantic bed-and-breakfast resort where they would spend their honeymoon. In order to keep the car in line with the camera truck, which led the way up the forested hillside, the young couple's convertible was towed behind the truck while the cameras shot through the car's windshield.

Kurt pretended to steer with his left hand. But his right repeatedly dropped out of camera range and wandered over to Christina's knee.

She ignored his rudeness for the first few takes. But when the crew stopped to adjust the angle of one of the cameras, she turned to him in her seat.

"I could concentrate on my lines a lot better if you kept your hands to yourself," she told him as nicely as she could through gritted teeth.

He tossed his head back and laughed. "Loosen up! If we take routine scenes like this too seriously, we'll both end up in the funny farm."

"Listen, this is my first film," she reminded him. "I don't want to mess up."

"Okay, okay!" He raised his hands in surrender. "We'll be all business until Ted calls it a day. How about dinner tonight? You must know some cool restaurants around here."

Christina frowned at him. He was so great-looking it was almost impossible not to melt when he flashed those blue eyes at her. But something about him, something deeper than his looks, gnawed at her. Maybe it was because he treated people as if they weren't really important, unless they did something he wanted, like give him a part in a movie or go out with him.

"Look," she began, trying to be patient, "thanks for the offer. But I have homework and—"

"Homework?" He stared at her in exaggerated disbelief, lifting one eyebrow just as he had for the poster of *Last Embrace*. She wondered if he was serious or acting a part now. "You're still in school?" he asked.

"I'm a senior, and I intend to graduate."

"Geez!" He smacked his forehead with the heel of his hand. "I'm sorry. I really am. But hey, you'll graduate. Don't sweat it. Think any principal in his right mind would let a teacher flunk you—a star in a major motion picture?"

"I think Mr. Hardy will personally sign me up for summer school if I screw up," she remarked dryly.

Kurt gazed at her glumly. "All right. No dinner tonight." Suddenly he brightened. "What about you dropping by my hotel after you're done with your schoolwork? We can study our lines for tomorrow."

She observed him dubiously as the makeup lady patted powder on her cheeks to soak up shiny spots. "No thanks."

Kurt stared at her, intrigued. "Let me guess—you have a boyfriend, and you're being faithful. Hey, that's cool."

"I don't have a boyfriend," she stated, her frustration building again. "But that shouldn't make any difference."

"No boyfriend? And you're brushing off Kurt Richmond?" Apparently he'd never been rejected by a girl before.

"My personal life is none of your business," Christina said brusquely as the car started to roll forward again. "The only relationship we have is strictly business."

That afternoon Kurt seemed to go out of his way to make Christina's life miserable. He deliberately muffed his lines on takes that she felt were her best, or else he cut in over her lines. He managed to miscue her several times, which made her look as if she didn't know what she was doing.

At the end of the workday, Dreising beckoned to them from behind one of the eight-foot-tall hedges that wound through the garden.

"I don't know what's going on between you two!" he growled under his breath. "You are supposed to be professionals. Ditch your personal problems while you're on camera!"

Kurt gazed into the treetops, managing to look bored.

With an exasperated grunt, Dreising turned to Christina. "Do you want to do this film or not?"

"Of course I do!" she blurted out, tears of frustration welling up in her eyes.

"Then forget about Christina English. Become Laura Merrick, your character! And you!" he shouted at Kurt. "Chill your hormones long enough to finish this film. Your agent said you need this role."

Kurt glared dangerously at Dreising. "I don't *need* any film, man. People are knocking my freakin' door down, begging me to star in their flicks."

"That's not what I hear, kid," Dreising sneered. "Shape up, or I'll find myself another star. I hear Michael Trevor is free."

Kurt's face turned bone-white. "He's not bad, but I'm a lot better."

"That's a matter of opinion," Dreising pronounced coldly.

The two glared fiercely at each other.

Christina stood by meekly, silently swallowing her tears. She longed to escape the crossfire of emotions zapping between the director and his star. She felt trapped in the middle of something menacing . . . something she had no hope of understanding . . . something that she sensed could destroy her dream of an acting career.

At last Dreising looked down at his hands and took a ragged breath, regaining control.

"Tomorrow's a big day," he said tightly. "We'll do the love scene in the woods. I want you both to go to bed tonight thinking cuddly thoughts about each other. Because, in the morning, I'll expect you to act like you're in love instead of tearing each other to shreds in front of the camera. Got it?"

"Yes, sir!" Christina answered quickly.

Kurt grumbled low in his throat and turned away.

Christina returned to her trailer, where she changed out of her costume and back into her own comfortable jeans. Her mind lingered on Kurt and Dreising's bitter argument as she opened the mini-fridge and took out a can of cream soda, her favorite drink. Only after she'd popped the tab and taken three long gulps of the cold, bubbly liquid did she begin to relax.

Tomorrow I'm going to act like I'm crazy in love with that egotistical jerk if it kills me! she thought.

The scene Dreising had spoken of, if played with anyone but Kurt, would have been pretty easy for her. Laura Merrick and her young husband Marty walk out of the castle, through the garden, and into the woods. Unknown to them, a moldy Sir Neville watches them kiss and reacts as if he's seeing his own bride of 100 years ago making love with a stranger. Predictably, his rage mounts until he can barely contain himself.

44

Simple.

Thankfully, the script called for nothing more than a bit of breathless love talk and a couple of tender kisses. All clothing would remain in place. But the thought of letting Kurt touch her at all made her skin crawl. She decided she'd have to work very hard tomorrow to keep her distaste for him from showing in her face.

Christina took another sip of the sweet vanilla soda and felt the last traces of tension seep out of her muscles.

It was at that moment that she noticed the script.

When she'd first entered the trailer, everything had seemed entirely normal, just as she'd left it. Now she noticed that her copy of *Dark Memories* lay on the cot.

Hadn't she left it on her dressing table?

Feeling a prickly sensation climb her spine, she slowly looked around the dressing room. Other subtle changes leaped out at her.

Before she'd left for the afternoon's work, she'd hung a couple of costumes that needed alterations on the curtain rod above the bed. In their place was another outfit—a filmy white gauze gown that resembled cobwebs. She was supposed to wear it in the final scenes when she was a zombie. Possibly one of the wardrobe people had picked up the first costumes and left the other. Possibly.

She looked around again. A cola can sat on her dressing table. She never drank cola. Had the same person who'd come for the costumes left it? And had that person picked up her script out of curiosity, then, forgetting where it had been, left it beneath the cobweb dress? Or was the arrangement of the two items intentional?

The gown looked ghostly, as if it were floating eerily in midair. Christina's hands began to tremble uncontrollably. Tiny hairs at the back of her neck stood at attention.

Someone has been here, she thought, wildly. But why?

45

Her fingers tingling, she reached down and fanned the script pages. A red paper marker was stuck between two pages. She stopped flipping and read the passage from the script:

EXT. THE GARDEN OUTSIDE THE CASTLE

Laura is in the coffin. Around it stand the mourners. The priest moves over beside Marty. He lowers the cover of the coffin.

MARTY: Good-bye, my sweet Laura. I loved you. I always will.

PRIEST: *Resting a hand on Marty's shoulder.* It's all right, son. She's at peace now.

CLOSE-UP OF COFFIN

Clods of dirt fall on lid. The layer of earth gets deeper and deeper.

Christina fingered the red bookmark, then turned it over. Written across it in jagged black letters were the words *And then you die!*

With a muffled whimper, Christina dropped the script and marker on her cot, backing away as if they'd bitten her.

"If this is a joke," she croaked out, "you've gone too far—whoever you are!"

Grabbing her purse and keys, she bolted from the trailer. She drove much too fast and didn't stop shaking all the way home.

Knowing that her parents were downstairs, Christina felt almost safe. But the lingering sensation of being tormented by a mysterious stranger never completely left her. She didn't tell them about the phone call or the bookmark. She was afraid that they might make her leave the film.

At nine o'clock her telephone rang, and she stared at it. She let it ring four times, expecting the answering machine to pick up. If it was the same person who'd left the message before and scribbled the threatening note in her script, she didn't want to give him the satisfaction of hearing her voice.

Unfortunately, she must have turned off the machine earlier. The phone continued ringing. Finally she thought the jangling bell would drive her crazy.

She picked up the receiver.

"Yes?" she whispered.

"Chris? This is John."

"Oh, hi!" she gasped, feeling like an idiot for being so hyper.

At least once a week he'd call and ask how she was—if anything new was going on in her life, that sort of thing. And he always told her how his ball games and track events had gone. He could talk about sports for hours. She didn't have much interest, but she listened as a friend.

"How are you?" she asked. "How was work today?"

"Super," he said cheerfully. "Dreising and Amanda kept me running all day. I was hoping to cut out and see them shoot a couple of your scenes, but there wasn't time. How did it go?"

"Well, a couple of scenes were pretty rocky," she admitted. "Kurt's being a real pain in the neck."

"How's that?"

"Oh—he hits on anything in a skirt."

John laughed. "That sure fits his reputation. I'm not surprised that it's the truth."

"Tomorrow's the love scene."

The line fell silent.

"You still there, John?"

47

"Yeah, sure. I, uh, I was just thinking that must be uncomfortable for you . . . I mean, kissing a guy you don't like."

"It'll be pretty weird."

"Maybe you can pretend he's someone else," he suggested.

She hadn't thought of that. But now that he mentioned it, it sounded like a pretty good idea. She wasn't sure who her fantasy lover should be, though. He should be someone who really appealed to her, someone exciting and mysterious. No one came to mind.

Suddenly she felt unbearably lonely. Other girls had boyfriends to call and chat with romantically for hours . . . to go on long sunny walks with . . . or just to hang out with at a friend's house. She had nobody. Nobody except some loony fan.

"Maybe I'll take your advice," she said at last. "I'd better go now. I have a lot to do tonight."

"Christina?" John hesitated as if he'd heard the strain in her voice. "Is something wrong?"

"No," she lied, not wanting to talk about her fears right before going to bed. She'd likely carry the terror into sleep, where it might flare into a nightmare.

"You sure? You sound tense."

"I'm fine, John. Thanks for calling."

"No sweat. Hey, listen, putting up with Kurt can't be that bad. Beryl would jump at the chance, if it meant getting the female lead."

"I shouldn't complain," she said quickly, feeling a little guilty. She hated whiners. The last thing she wanted was to become one. "Well, good night."

"Good night, Chris."

Christina hung up and gazed thoughtfully around her room. John was right. What she needed was some guy other than Kurt to focus on. Some face she could imagine hovering tenderly over her, kissing her gently on the lips. She grabbed the stack of magazines beside her bed and

48

flipped through one, then another and another.

All the faces of familiar male stars and models were handsome and smiled invitingly at her. But they were plastic smiles, the kind she'd learned to give the camera. Tossing the magazines aside, Christina reached into the bottom drawer of her dresser for last year's yearbook. She turned to the section of photographs of her classmates.

At least these people were real. Most of them she knew by sight, if not by name. Her finger raced along the rows.

Some of the guys were immediate turnoffs, and she eliminated them right away. They were mean to other students or prided themselves on making lousy grades, because they thought that was cool. Some were into heavy drinking or smoked like chimneys—both very uncool habits as far as she was concerned. Once she'd narrowed down the field, she got serious about appearance.

Christina liked dark-haired guys—maybe because she was fair. She eliminated blonds and redheads.

At last, her finger paused at a serious, square-jawed face. The boy looked straight into the camera as if he were fearless. His eyes seemed to reach out to her. There was a pleasant crinkle at the corners of his mouth, as if he smiled a lot but had chosen not to at the moment the photo had been shot. An interesting tingle feathered through her stomach, and she smiled softly.

"You," she murmured, recalling his name before she read the caption. *Steve Jackson. Wrestling team. Nickname: Doomsday. Honor student. Yearbook committee. Photography Club. Young Engineers.*

He wasn't her type at all. A jock, and a smart one. But there was something . . . something fascinating about him. She found it difficult, almost impossible actually, to look away from his picture. He'd asked her out once. She'd wanted to go out with him, but she'd had a shoot scheduled out of town for that weekend. She'd been a little sorry when he never asked her out again.

Christina shut her eyes and leaned back into her pillow, wrapping her arms cozily around the yearbook. Yes, she could easily conjure up Steve's strong features. She would think of him when Kurt kissed her. Already she felt warmer and happier inside than she had in months.

When Steve woke up it took him a good ten minutes to remember he didn't have to go to school that day because it was Saturday. No wrestling practice or meet scheduled either. If he liked, he could sleep all day.

Then he remembered about *Dark Memories* . . . and Christina.

He flung the covers off of his bed and dressed in his sweats as if he were heading out for his usual five-mile run. It was seven o'clock in the morning, but he knew movie crews started early. He wanted to be at the castle by the time Christina arrived.

The sweats would give him an excuse for jogging through the state park. Once he got close, the gray fleece would blend with the tree bark and shadows. With luck he'd be able to watch for a while before someone chased him off. He tucked his 35-mm camera securely into the hand-warmer pouch on the front of his sweatshirt and safety-pinned the ends shut.

The park was close to six miles from Steve's house. He ran it in about fifty minutes, and wasn't even short of breath when he turned off the narrow approach road and into the woods. He thought, *If Christina sees me, maybe I'll tell her to her face what a great fan of hers I am. Then I can ask her if she'd like to go for a pizza after she's done for the day.*

However, he suspected, like all the other times, he'd never work up his courage. What would she want with a guy like him . . . when she had Kurt Richmond?

A bitter taste filled his mouth, and he felt a frustrated rage building inside his chest. He stopped running and leaned his forehead against a tree. With a sudden violent surge of energy, he drew back a fist and punched the trunk. He stared down at his scuffed knuckles as they turned purple. For a moment the pain in his hand took his mind off of the pain in his heart. He started walking up the hill.

Fresh determination settled over Steve as he climbed through the woods. This time he wasn't going to take no for an answer. He would get her attention . . . somehow. He'd talk to her and *make* her like him.

Christina shut her eyes for a moment, pressing her back against the rough bark of a convenient tree trunk, rehearsing her lines in her head.

In a way, she thought, movies were easier than plays. In a live performance you had to know every line cold, from the first of act one to the last of act three. If you made a mistake, you couldn't stop and repeat a line or a bit of action until you got it right.

But while filming a movie, the action was broken up into thousands of brief shots. An actor might deliver only two or three lines before the director shouted, "Cut!" Then, while grips repositioned cameras and equipment and shifted scenery, the cast could review their next lines. In fact, there often was too much dead time between shots. It gave her time to dwell on the wrong things— like her mysterious fan.

I'm going to think of Steve, she thought nervously as a makeup assistant touched up her lipstick.

Although kissing a boy had always seemed great fun, to do it with nearly a hundred people watching—well, that was weird. Even more unsettling was the fear that her psycho fan might be somewhere in the audience.

"Somebody find Kurt!" Dreising shouted. "We're ready."

Christina stepped up to her mark and looked around, aware that everyone was watching her. After all, she was the newcomer and Kurt's latest costar. They'd probably already placed bets on whether she was sleeping with him . . . yet.

Well, she thought with a wicked grin, *they're going to have a very long wait.*

At last Kurt showed up. He looked out of breath and flushed. A guy from makeup descended on him before he'd stepped in front of the cameras.

"I thought I told you to stay close!" Dreising snapped.

"I'm here, aren't I?" Kurt demanded hotly. He pushed the powder brush away. "Let's get this over with."

Christina stared at him. Yesterday he had been all over her. This morning he seemed to dread this scene as much as she did.

"All right, kids," Dreising began doubtfully. "Remember, you're crazy about each other. You're newlyweds, and this is your first night together as husband and wife."

Christina turned to face Kurt. As she did, out of the corner of her eyes, she glimpsed a stray motion, something beyond the waves of faces of the crew who were standing statue-still. But, as suddenly as it had appeared, it was gone. She looked up at Kurt.

His stony glare from a moment earlier had transformed into an adoring smile. She could almost believe that he loved her . . . almost, but not quite. She knew him too well. Perhaps he was a better actor than she'd thought.

"Action!" snapped Dreising. He hunched over in his canvas chair, chin propped on his fist.

I'm doing this in one take, Christina told herself. *Think of the smart jock. Think of Steve Jackson and forget you're kissing this conceited Romeo.*

Slowly, Christina melted against Kurt's chest. She lifted her arms up around his neck as his hands closed around her waist.

"I love you, babe," he murmured his opening line. "I don't know what I would do if you disappeared from my life."

"I love you too," she cooed convincingly.

He bent over her, and she could feel his breath trace across her cheek toward her lips. She closed her eyes, conjuring up Steve's sturdy face and honest brown eyes. Christina felt lips cover hers. Again she thought of Steve, pressing his lips softly over hers.

For a few golden seconds, she convinced herself that the boy in the yearbook was actually there with her. She didn't object when Kurt's kiss deepened. It was as if he and everyone else around them had evaporated into the spring air. She and Kurt were alone in a beautiful wooded park. The pine needles smelled sweet. Birds twittered approvingly in the treetops.

Suddenly, she was aware that something was wrong. Her eyes popped open, and she stared suspiciously at Kurt's mischievously twinkling eyes. A breeze tickled her stomach.

Immediately, her eyes dropped to find only one button holding her blouse closed.

"You pervert!" she shrieked. "That's not in the script!"

Kurt laughed uproariously.

Dreising bellowed, "Cut!" He stalked toward them. "What the hell's your problem, you two?"

"*He's* the problem!" Christina cried furiously. "We were supposed to kiss, not undress each other!"

Kurt rolled his eyes innocently. "She was responding to me. I ad-libbed a little. No big deal."

Christina glared at him, then spun to face Dreising. "I wasn't ready for that. I—"

The director of photography interrupted. "Forget it, Ted. Either she was really enjoying herself or acting extremely well. We have some great footage."

Dreising grinned.

Christina blushed. "Then we don't have to do it again?" she asked weakly.

"No. This take was a keeper," Dreising said, his mood notably improved. "Listen, from now on just relax and

53

let Kurt charm you like just now. It worked great." He winked at her, then walked away.

"I'd rather eat goat turd," she muttered.

Kurt snickered. "If I get too hot for you, babe, we can always find another actress who can handle Laura's part." Suddenly, his expression turned serious. He stepped closer to her, and his voice sank to a taut whisper. "No girl snubs *me* and gets away with it. You're gonna pay, sweetheart."

Chapter 5

Christina cringed at the viciousness in Kurt's voice. As she watched him storm off, she thought of the bookmark. Could he have left it and the spooky dress as a way of gloating over her pretend death? She found it hard to believe any guy would get that steamed just because a girl refused to date him.

On the other hand, she thought grimly, *Kurt does have a King Kong ego.*

But what about the message on her answering machine? It had been left the day she'd met him. She hadn't done anything to crush his ego then. Could two different people be behind the incidents?

At the end of the day, Christina spotted Beryl standing with a couple of other extras near the trailers. At least she supposed it must be her classmate under a ton of theatrical makeup. Beryl had been skillfully transformed into a teenage slut, complete with skintight leopard-print bodysuit, leather miniskirt, tacky jewelry, and platinum wig.

"Hi," Christina greeted her wearily. "How's it going?" She was glad that the day was almost over. It was seven o'clock, getting dark. She was starving and her nerves were worn to the breaking point.

Beryl scowled and turned away.

"What's the matter?" Christina asked.

"Nothing." Beryl tipped her nose in the air. "Nothing at all." Then she turned back, her eyes glistening with tears. "Good grief, are you blind? Look what they did to me! All my friends will see me in the movie, looking like a . . . a hooker or something! This skirt is so short I might as well not be wearing it! And these fake eyelashes and goop all over my face . . . It's disgusting!"

Christina swallowed a laugh. Beryl did look pretty outrageous. "Don't feel bad. They're going to *kill* me tomorrow."

For a second, Beryl looked perplexed, then she smiled unsteadily. "Oh, you mean in the script. Dreising's shooting the death scene tomorrow?"

"The funeral. I'll have to sit through three hours of makeup prep to look like a corpse."

"Gross," Beryl admitted. "But at least you're the star, and they make you look fantastic for the first half of the movie." She sighed wistfully. "I'm never going to be anything more than an extra."

"Your turn will come," Christina said encouragingly, putting an arm around Beryl's shoulders. As tired as she was and preoccupied with her own problems, she felt sorry for the other girl.

"You sound like my mother," Beryl grumbled. "Just last night she told me that when I least expect it, I'll get the big break I need. What does she know?"

"I'm sure she's right. Just keep working at it," Christina recommended.

Beryl shrugged off Christina's arm and glared at her. "I will, you can bet on that. I'd . . . I'd absolutely *kill* for a part like yours."

Christina shifted her feet. "Hey," she laughed uneasily, "I think we both need to chill out. It's been a rough day. Are you done?"

"Yeah. Why?" Beryl asked suspiciously as she started pulling hairpins from her wig.

"Come to my trailer and clean up," Christina offered. "We can grab a couple of burgers at Mike's on our way home and eat them at my place."

Beryl shook her head. "No thanks. I gotta stop and pick up some milk and bread for my mother."

"We can do that together," Christina said hastily.

Suddenly she was terrified at the thought of going home to an empty house. She wanted someone to be with her when she walked in the door. She wanted someone to help her check under the beds, make sure none of the windows had been jimmied open from the outside, search the house for cruel notes. Beryl in the midst of a rotten mood might not be ideal company, but she was better than nothing.

"Please?" Christina pleaded.

"Honest," Beryl insisted, giving her a strange look, as if spooked by Christina's persistence. She hurriedly backed away. "I have a lot of homework and a dance lesson. Not tonight. Maybe another time."

Christina sighed and looked around. Almost everyone else in the cast had cleared out by now. They were all as exhausted and hungry as she was. Only a few technicians remained, locking up expensive camera equipment for the night.

Christina climbed the wooden steps to her dressing room, opened the metal door, and looked cautiously around the dim interior. Everything seemed as she'd left it—her jeans, shoes, and sweatshirt laid out neatly on the cot, her script beside them, the chair to the dressing table pulled out at a slight angle the way she would have left it. Puffing out her cheeks, she blew a shallow breath of relief and turned on the light.

It took only a fraction of a second for her eyes to focus on the mirror. In the dark, its reflection hadn't caught her attention. But in the glow of the bulbs surrounding her mirror . . .

57

Her throat felt as if it were closing up. She gulped back her terror.

Written in dripping letters of blood across the silvery glass were the words:

TOMORROW YOU DIE!

For a dozen heartbeats Christina stared at the streaks covering her mirror. Strangely mesmerized by the crimson smears, she stepped toward the glass. She touched one finger to the letter T. Her fingertip came away wet and red.

The sour taste of bile filled her mouth, and she swayed violently before the mirror. Before her knees could buckle, Christina staggered to the door and latched it, then dashed for the bathroom. She soaked a washcloth in the sink and returned to the mirror to swipe at the letters.

All her frantic efforts did was streak the surface, making it seem as if there were even more blood seeping through the mirror from some gory source behind the glass. Liquid dripped down her arm, creating bright crimson splotches on her makeup jars.

Tears fogged Christina's vision. Clenching her teeth, she refused to cry. Whoever was playing these awful tricks on her was *not* going to get to her. If this was another of Kurt's ploys to bully her into dating him— she'd strangle him with her bare hands! If it were someone else, she'd show him she couldn't be scared off by—

A knock sounded on her door.

Her hand reacted by tightening on the washcloth, squeezing out a stream of diluted blood over her dressing table. She dropped the cloth and stared at the door.

The next knock was louder. The third rattled the metal door.

Christina swallowed, her mind whirling. What should she do? Ignore it? Pretend she wasn't here? But her light was on, and anyone watching the trailer would have seen her come in.

"Who is it?" she rasped out, the words burning her throat.

"You don't know me. I go to Hanover High."

She drew half of a breath. Maybe her demented fan had decided to show himself.

The door was already locked. She could call security. One man remained on duty all night to keep an eye on valuable equipment and props.

"I just want to talk to you for a minute," the voice said. "Please."

Something about that last word soothed her torn nerves. A polite psycho didn't make sense. She unlocked the door, and there stood Steve Jackson.

"Hi," he said bashfully.

"Hi," she returned.

The same boy she'd fantasized about during her love scene with Kurt. She felt her cheeks glow pink with embarrassing heat. But it was reassuring to know that Steve couldn't possibly realize she'd picked him out of the yearbook. And she'd never, never tell him.

The actress in her took over. She made her voice sound unemotional, a little bored. "What do you want?"

Despite her cool greeting, Steve smiled and the skin at the corners of his lips crinkled just as affably as she'd guessed it would. "I was jogging through the park grounds this morning and lost my watch. I didn't realize it was missing until tonight. Drove back to see if someone on the crew found it."

"Did they?"

He shook his head. "Most everyone is gone. I didn't get to ask anyone. Then I saw that your car was still here and—Hey, is anything wrong?"

Later, she wondered why she decided to confide in him. Maybe because he sounded so timid, he made her feel braver. Maybe because he looked so strong, filling out his T-shirt as he filled up her doorway. She thought, *If he's not my psycho, he'll make a fantastic bodyguard!* Or maybe she just felt naturally close to him. After all, they'd already kissed—at least in her imagination.

"Come in." She surprised herself by reaching out into the dusk to pull him up the steps by his arm.

He blinked, letting his eyes adjust to the light. "This is nice," he commented.

"It would be nicer if a certain creep would leave me alone," she groaned.

Steve frowned. "Someone's bothering you?"

"The other night I came home to find a message on my answering machine. Somebody claiming to be my greatest fan. But the voice said if I disappointed him or her, I'd regret it."

"You're kidding!"

"No." She started pacing the tiny space between her cot and dressing table. "And yesterday someone broke into my trailer and left another message in my script."

"I take it that it wasn't 'Break a leg'?"

"No such luck."

Steve's eyes darkened. He looked around the room warily. His glance stopped at the dripping washrag on her dressing table. It had been white. It was now a gruesome shade of pink.

"Did you cut yourself?" he asked with concern.

Christina raised her right hand in front of her face. Blood stained the spaces between her fingers.

"Just trying to clean up. My phantom fan struck again tonight," she whispered hoarsely. "He wrote on my mirror—'Tomorrow you die!' "

"In *blood?*"

"Looks like it."

Steve stepped up to the mirror to observe the remaining red streaks. "You should call the police and report this. A stranger who telephones his favorite actress once is probably harmless. He might have thought he was

60

encouraging you to do well. But . . . but this—" He hesitated, looking at her solemnly. "The guy could be dangerous. Remember that soap-opera star who was stalked by a fan a couple of years ago? He eventually killed her."

"Thanks for that pleasant thought," Christina remarked dryly.

Steve shrugged, as if to say, *I can't help the way the world is.*

Then he turned his attention back to the dressing table. With one outstretched finger he touched a red glob on the cap of a jar of powder. Bringing his finger up to his nose, he sniffed, then touched it gingerly to the tip of his tongue.

"Geez!" she shrieked. "Don't *do* that!"

Steve grinned ghoulishly at her. "Afraid I might turn into a vampire?"

"Of course not, it's just too gross to—"

"This isn't blood," he explained quickly. "It tastes sweet. Like syrup."

Now that he mentioned it, she thought he probably was right. "FX specialists make their own fake blood," she murmured, then looked up at Steve. "Gus, the head of Dreising's makeup team, told me one very simple recipe—clear Karo syrup with red and yellow food coloring."

"That's probably what this is," Steve said. "But that doesn't mean whoever's behind these stunts isn't dangerous." He looked at her steadily. "I should drive you home. As soon as we get there, you tell your parents what's up and see if they don't agree you should call the police."

Christina hesitated. "If I leave my car, how will I get back here tomorrow morning?"

He looked away for a moment, then back into her eyes. "Listen, Chris, are you sure you *want* to come back?"

"Huh?"

He took a deep breath. "Let's face it, someone's going

to a lot of trouble to scare you off the film. You don't know how far they'll go. Is keeping this role worth risking your life?"

"Nothing can make me quit," she ground out.

He nodded slowly, as if the words took a while to sink in. "I guess you have to do what you have to do," he murmured. "How about I pick you up in the morning and deliver you to work. What time?"

"I have a six A.M. makeup call."

"I'll be there at five-thirty," he promised.

After Steve dropped her off at her house, Christina barely got out half of her story before her father stopped her with one raised hand.

"We're calling the authorities," he stated gruffly.

"I agree," her mother said quickly.

Two officers from the Connecticut state police arrived in less than twenty minutes. The one who seemed to be in charge was middle-aged, his belly bulging a bit over his belt as if he liked beer when he was off duty. His partner was tall, young, and had a nice smile beneath a neat reddish mustache.

The five of them went into the living room and sat down.

Christina started from the beginning, explaining as she had to Steve about the message on her answering machine, the note in her script, and the three chilling words scrawled across her mirror.

The older police officer never took his eyes off of Christina's face as she spoke. "Can we hear this tape, miss?" he asked when she had finished.

"I erased the message," she admitted. At the time she'd assumed it was a freak call, an isolated incident. How was she to know it was the beginning of a nightmare?

"What about the bookmark and mirror?" he asked.

"I wiped the blood off the mirror." She thought for a moment, unable to recall what she'd done with the bookmark. "I suppose the other note is still at the trailer with my script. I should have brought it home to study tomorrow's lines, but I was pretty shook up and didn't think to bring it."

The older cop turned to his partner. "Drive on over to the park. See if you can find the bookmark in Miss English's trailer."

He continued to question Christina about the filming location. Were the trailers locked? At night, yes. But sometimes, during the day when she was running in and out between scenes, she'd leave the door open so that she wouldn't have to carry keys. Did the public have access to the castle grounds? No, they did not.

Fifteen minutes into his inquisition, the phone rang.

Four pairs of eyes fixed on it.

"Please answer that, sir," the officer directed her father.

Mr. English stood and crossed to the phone.

"English residence," he pronounced tightly. Almost at once, his expression eased. "It's for you," he said, handing the officer the receiver.

"What you got?" the man asked. "Yeah . . . you sure? She said red . . . probably stuck it in the script. All right, come on back."

As soon as he'd hung up, he lifted his head to study Christina through narrowed eyes. "My sergeant can't find any bookmark anywhere in the trailer."

"Are you sure he looked everywhere?" Christina demanded.

"He's very good at looking everywhere," the officer said dryly. He turned his back on her. "Mr. and Mrs. English, may I speak with Christina alone for a moment?"

Her father looked at her. His pale eyes, mirror images of hers, looked as worried as they had on another night, long ago. She'd run a hundred-and-four-degree fever. He'd rushed her to the emergency room, and the doctor

63

had admitted her into the hospital for three days.

"If that's all right with her," her father said.

She nodded.

When her parents had left the living room, the officer stood up, walked over to look out the window into the dark, and cleared his throat.

"I don't want you to take this the wrong way, young lady. Just listen to me first."

Christina had no idea what he was preparing to say. "I will," she promised, looking up at him from the couch.

"I'd guess this movie means a lot to you," he said.

"It does."

"And you'd do anything to make a success of it—this one being your first?"

"I'll work as hard as I can," she said.

"When there's a lot of publicity about a movie before it hits the theaters—that makes a big difference, doesn't it?" He turned around and leveled bloodshot eyes at her. "I mean, if some kind of exciting news leaks out and the press get hold of it, they write articles. Then the public gets curious and buys more tickets. Am I right?"

Christina frowned, feeling the need to be cautious. "Yes. But I'm not sure what you're trying to say."

"I'm talking about rigging a publicity stunt," he snapped at her. "Say an actress in a horror movie is being stalked by some loony fan. All of a sudden, the film's getting free press, coast-to-coast!"

Christina leaped up from the couch. "I wouldn't do that!" she shouted.

The cop leaned his heavy rump against the windowsill and observed her coldly. "We don't *know* that. Besides, it might not be you. Can you think of anyone else involved in the film who might pull something like this? Someone who wouldn't mind using you to get publicity?"

"Absolutely not!" she retorted. But even as the words escaped her lips, names flashed through her head. Names she didn't want to think about now, not while she was upset.

The police officer watched her expression shift from anger to doubt. "Think about it," he said, walking over to her. "Meanwhile, keep an eye on your trailer. If something else happens, save the evidence." He took out his wallet, pulled a card from it, and handed it to her. "Call me if this joker shows up again."

"Will you be investigating in the meantime?" she asked hopefully.

He rubbed a plump thumb thoughtfully across his chin. "If this harassment continues, and we're sure this isn't some Hollywood gimmick . . ."

A lump clogged her throat. "I *am* sure," she breathed.

He gave her a long, considering look. "We'll see."

The next morning Steve picked up Christina in his vintage 1971 Pinto. The yellow paint had long ago faded to a dirty cream. Tan vinyl seats were shredded and held together with dark-brown plastic tape. Behind her seat, a rust hole had developed in the floor. She wondered how far they could safely drive before she found herself sitting in the road.

However, none of that mattered. She was just thankful she didn't have to drive up to the castle alone.

Strapping herself in, she smiled at Steve. "Thanks for doing this. Getting up before six on a Sunday morning is a drag."

"No problem." He flashed her a friendly grin. "Anytime you want a chauffeur, just call."

She nodded and looked out the window as they drove out of town, turned north along the Connecticut River, and headed toward the state park. The morning was fog-enshrouded, a damp and bone-chilling gray.

"Dreising will love this weather if it lasts," she commented.

"Huh?"

She turned to look at Steve. His neck above the blue stripe on his T-shirt was thick and muscled. She figured that was a result of his wrestling, and the training that must go along with it. Boys who looked like Steve had always frightened her and made her feel vulnerable. Somehow she didn't feel that way this morning.

"The fog . . . no sun," she explained. "If this pea soup doesn't burn off by ten o'clock, he'll be ecstatic. We're shooting my funeral today."

Steve laughed. "If I didn't know we were talking make-believe, I'd be shaking."

"I'm shaking, movie or not. I don't like pretending to die, not like this with all the blood and gore. It's too real."

He glanced sideways at her. "Are you sure you want to go through with this?"

"I have to. This is my chance to be in a major motion picture. Acting is what I want to do more than anything in the world."

He nodded. "I guess I know what it's like to want something that bad." He was silent for several minutes. The mists seemed to part for the jouncing car as it rumbled up the highway. After a while, Steve continued. "Sometimes when I'm wrestling, I think to myself— this is all that matters, this match, these five minutes. It's as if everything depends on my taking down my opponent."

"You're really serious about wrestling," she commented, observing him with interest.

He shrugged. "At least when I'm in the middle of a match. I guess life is sort of like that. When you get involved in something, it seems like the world will end if you screw up. Right now . . . well, wrestling doesn't seem so special, even with regionals coming up next week." His gaze drifted beyond the windshield, toward a distant spot in the fog. "There are other more important things."

Christina slid down in her seat, enjoying the sound of his deep voice. "Like what?"

Steve looked startled, as if he suddenly realized he'd spoken out loud. He watched the road intently, too intently—as if he were using the task of driving to avoid looking at her.

Without warning, a car pulled out of a blind driveway. Steve slammed on his brakes and swerved to the right, narrowly avoiding the vehicle's tail end.

Christina gripped the door handle, bracing herself with both feet as they skittered to a stop on the shoulder, pebbles flying from beneath the wheels.

The sedan didn't even slow down. In another moment, it had disappeared over the next rise.

For several seconds, neither of them said a word. As crazily as her own heart pounded in her chest, she was certain she heard Steve's thudding like a jackhammer.

"That was close," he breathed at last.

"Thank goodness for an athlete's reflexes." She rubbed the knotted muscles at the backs of her legs. "I don't think I could have stopped in time."

"I'm sure you would have," he said. Nevertheless, he looked pleased with her compliment. "Hey, I have an idea—how about I hang out at the set for a while? You know, just to make sure no one bothers you."

Automatically, she opened her mouth to tell him no. Then she realized she liked the idea of his being close by. It would be comforting to think that someone as strong and capable as Steve was looking after her.

"Getting you onto the set might be a little sticky," she said slowly. "If you don't mind, I could tell Dreising you're my boyfriend. That might also shut down Kurt's hormones for a while."

"You mean Kurt Richmond?"

"Yeah." She laughed, shaking her head. "The guy lives up to his reputation. If he thinks I have a serious relationship with someone else, maybe he'll cool it."

"I don't mind being used." Steve grinned from ear-to-ear as he pulled the car back onto the highway. "Maybe we should, you know, hold hands or something to make it look good."

Christina smiled, feeling happily light-headed at his suggestion. "Why not?"

Chapter 6

It was early on Sunday morning. Foggy and damp, with a sinister chill in the air, the day seemed perfect for the dark deed planned for this day. The lone figure in the basement room flipped a book open to the page of instructions marked by a strip of red construction paper.

In a way, it was unfortunate that Christina had to be eliminated by such violent means. All she'd had to do to save herself was quit the film. Everything would have been perfect then.

However, nothing had worked. Not the message on the answering machine, not the nasty bookmark and ghostly dress, or the warning in blood on her mirror. Now, all that remained was a more drastic solution.

Carefully, fingers twisted a short piece of thread-like wire. The tiny detonator cap would fit in the crease beneath the paper flap. When Christina tore open the envelope, there would be a fraction of a second's delay—then the explosion.

With her hands and face so close to the letter bomb when it went off . . . well—a satisfied smirk spread over taut lips—no photographer would ever pay her to pose for a camera again. The only question that remained was how and when to deliver the final message.

Steve took Christina's hand as they started up the steep path from the state park's parking area, a half mile below the castle. At the security guard's shack, Christina introduced Steve as her boyfriend. The man on duty waved them through with a smile.

They'd almost reached Christina's trailer when they ran into Amanda.

She raised her hand in absentminded greeting to Christina. Then her glance shifted to Steve. "Who's your friend?" she asked sternly.

"This is my guy Steve," Christina announced cheerfully. "Steve, this is Amanda Perry, Mr. Dreising's assistant."

Amanda's eyes narrowed suspiciously. "At your audition you said you didn't have a boyfriend."

Christina sighed dramatically and clung to Steve's arm. "We'd had a fight. You know how it is."

"But now we're back together again," Steve chimed in, pulling Christina cozily to his side.

"Oh?" Amanda paused, studying them as if she didn't quite believe what she was seeing. "You're here awfully early, Christina."

"Makeup for the funeral."

"That's right. I'd forgotten." Amanda gave her a strained grin. "Well—I don't envy you, sitting for three hours while Gus plasters you with goop. Oh, before I go . . . I have some mail for you." She pulled an envelope out from under her clipboard. "Looks like a fan letter."

"Thanks," Christina said, studying the address on the plain white envelope:

Christina English
c/o Dark Memories Production Company

There was no return address. No postmark. Someone must have delivered it in person to the guard shack.

The handwriting was spiky, slanting first one way then the other, and smudged, as if the writer had been in a hurry.

A chill inched up each joint of her spine.

Steve must have felt her tense up against his arm. "Anything wrong?" he asked as soon as Amanda left.

"I . . . I don't know," she stammered, her stomach clenching nervously. She turned over the envelope. It looked as if it had been opened, then resealed. She wondered fleetingly if Amanda really did read the cast's mail, searching for the least sign of treason to Dreising. But something much more important was on her mind. "I think this might be another . . . you know."

"A threat?" He reacted immediately. "I'll open it for you, if you like."

She thrust the letter at him as if it were a red-hot chunk of charcoal. Standing back, she watched as Steve slipped his wide thumb beneath the flap and sliced open the envelope. He slowly withdrew a sheet of dirty notepaper between two fingers. As he opened it, a grin spread over his face.

"What?" she demanded, moving closer to peer over his shoulder.

"Listen to this. 'My name is Paula Smith. I am in Mrs. Oliver's third grade class. I live in Hanover just like you. I read about you in the newspaper. Someday I want to be a famous actress just like you.' "

The spasms in Christina's stomach relaxed. She took a deep breath. "I'm starting to imagine things, aren't I? Sorry."

"You can't help being scared," Steve said sympathetically. "You don't know who's your friend and who's your enemy."

Are you my friend, Steve? she mused. *I mean, really my friend?* Or was he just being nice to her for the same reason the third-grader had written that letter—because she was in a movie. Because someday she might be famous.

"I'd better get going," she murmured, dropping her eyes away from his.

"Yeah." But his hand shot out, gently holding her back. "Listen, if it'll make you feel better, I'll hang out at your trailer for a while, keep an eye on it for you. In a couple of hours, I'll stop by and see how your makeup's coming."

"I'd like that," she said cautiously.

As Christina walked away, tucking the letter into her purse, she actually started to hum. Maybe she had a chance this time. Maybe beneath his big-jock exterior, Steve was just a nice guy who liked her for herself.

By seven-thirty, Gus Murphy had succeeded in making Christina look worse than she'd ever looked in her entire eighteen years. That included the time she'd been in the hospital with pneumonia.

By using latex and skin-colored putty, he'd built up the flesh around her eyes and nose, which in turn made her eyes and cheeks appear hollow. Painstakingly working layers of makeup over this base, he tinted her new skin a bluish-white with gray mottling. Then he'd helped her put in contact lenses that dulled her blue eyes to a flat, lifeless gray.

When Christina stared at herself in the mirror, she felt as dead as she looked.

"Of course, in the coffin you won't need the contacts," he explained. "Your eyes will be shut."

She fought back the impulse to push Gus and his assistant aside, run to the sink, and wash the horrid mess away. She told herself that some people would get a charge out of going through the transformation from the living world to that of the dead.

But she couldn't shake the dreadful feeling that she was straddling a fragile line. Only fate knew where and when Christina Ann English would breathe her last breath. It seemed bad luck to mock Death, as if to say, *I'm not afraid of you—so there!* Just as the demented Sir Neville had challenged his own fate.

She looked up miserably when Steve poked his head around the corner and stared at her.

"Chris?" he asked, unsure.

"It's me, unfortunately," she muttered.

Gus jerked his head up. "Don't talk, love. You'll crack the latex before it's dry."

Gus had grown up in England and called everyone "love." He sounded like Paul McCartney and even resembled an aging Beatle with his bowl-cut hair. Now he was applying undertaker's rouge to her cheeks.

"Sorry," she breathed, without moving her lips.

"You want me to go?" Steve asked. His eyes darted nervously around the room, as if he wanted to say something but was unable to with Gus and his assistant in the room.

She wondered if something had happened back at the trailer.

Stay, her eyes told him. *Please stay*. She looked at him questioningly.

"Everything's fine at your dressing room," he said, reading her mind.

So—what was wrong? She wriggled in her seat, eaten up with curiosity.

"Sit still," Gus cautioned. "This your boyfriend?"

Gus knew everyone on the set. A film company was a close family, she was learning. Outsiders stood out and weren't generally welcome.

"Yes," Christina managed to whisper while keeping her face immobile.

Steve introduced himself. "You must be Gus Murphy. Christina told me you were the best makeup artist in the business."

Gus beamed at Christina, then glanced back at Steve

while he continued to work. "Got a great profile, kid. You an actor?"

"Naw. Chris and I just go to the same high school. I'm more into sports than movies."

Gus looked interested. "Hey, really? Which sports?"

"Wrestling mostly."

"He's last year's regional and state champ," Christina blurted out, ignoring Gus's rule about speaking.

Steve looked surprised and pleased that she knew about his record.

"Shhhh!" Gus shook a warning finger at her, but seemed more interested in finding out about Steve than keeping her quiet. "No kidding! My boy back in L.A., he's a freshman and a wrestler too. 'Course he's just a featherweight, a hundred and three pounds dripping wet. He wrestles JV."

The two of them talked for almost an hour while Gus made Christina look increasingly more disgusting. Every once in a while, Steve made a ridiculous face at her to try to make her laugh.

She listened to Steve as Gus worked. He told the makeup artist all about his wrestling and his plans to use athletics to win himself a scholarship.

"I want to be a sports therapist, someone who works with professional and amateur athletes. When an athlete is injured he or she often needs special treatment and retraining to return to full capacity before injury."

By the time her makeup was complete, Christina felt as if she'd known Steve for years. He cared about people and had been kind to her. She liked him now even more than she'd liked him when he'd been a stranger in her yearbook.

When at last they walked out of the makeup trailer into the cloudy day, Steve looked as if he were having trouble not laughing.

"Don't even think about making some crack about how lovely I look," she mumbled through gritted teeth,

74

although she knew she couldn't blame him if he did.

"Wouldn't think of it, Morticia!" he replied with a perfectly straight face.

"That does it!" she shrieked in mock rage. Laughing out loud, she seized a cushion from one of the crew's stools and clobbered him over the head with it.

He laughed, seizing her wrists. His hold was firm, but she could tell that he was being careful not to hurt her. She sensed that he was incredibly strong. If he wanted to, he could snap her wrists simply by applying a quick pressure with his thumbs on the fragile bones. But he was playing gently—and she loved it. She wondered if sometime he'd pretend-wrestle with her. That might be fun.

The thought of Steve pinning her made her feel happily short of breath. She shrieked and fought him for the cushion.

"Christina!" barked a commanding voice.

Steve immediately released her, and they both swung around.

Dreising stood between two trailers, feet planted wide apart, fists shoved down on his hips. He scowled darkly, gray rings of fatigue beneath his eyes. Beside him stood Kurt.

"Mr. Dreising!" Christina gasped. "Hi. We were just—"

"Do you have any idea how much that makeup you're wearing costs this production company?" he asked.

"Well, no. I, uh—"

"Plenty, let me tell you. But worse than that, if Gus has to start all over because you've messed it up, your thoughtlessness will delay the day's shooting schedule another three hours. I'll have to pay a camera crew time and a half for standing around on a Sunday morning."

"I'm sorry," she murmured.

Kurt stared curiously at Steve. Following his star's gaze, Dreising seemed to notice the stranger for the first time.

"Who are you?" he demanded.

"I'm with Chris," Steve answered quickly, sensing she was flustered and might unintentionally blow his cover. He grasped her hand.

"I wasn't aware that Chris had a boyfriend," Dreising said, looking him over closely.

"Me either," Kurt muttered, skeptically.

"My Chrissy's not much of a talker." Steve slung a thick arm around her and hugged her. "Guess she saves all her lines for the camera."

"Does she," Dreising mused, still looking suspicious.

Christina hastily changed the subject to take their minds off Steve. "Have the police contacted you yet?"

The director looked startled. "Police? Why would the police call me?"

"Some jerk has been harassing Chris," Steve explained. "Leaving threatening messages."

Christina wondered if he'd intentionally omitted mentioning what the messages were and how they were left. Perhaps he too wondered if Dreising had anything to do with them.

She remembered the police officer accusing her of trying to create publicity. When she'd flatly denied it, he'd asked her if anyone else involved in *Dark Memories* might be tempted to use her to get press for the film. She'd thought a lot about that question.

Dreising was the obvious suspect, since he'd sunk a fortune of his own money in the movie. Amanda Perry would cross the Mojave Desert barefoot if she thought that would help Dreising. And there were hundreds of others—investors, agents, studio executives—whose futures were linked with the success of *Dark Memories*.

But now she recalled something she'd read in *Variety*. Rumor had it that Kurt had closed a very sweet deal when he'd signed on with the picture. He'd agreed to take less money up front in favor of points at the box

76

office. That meant if the movie did well, he'd be rolling in cash since he'd earn a percentage of the ticket profits. However, if it bombed, he'd lose big. It was a huge gamble.

Yes, she thought grimly as she clung to Steve's hand, *he'll want to get as much attention for this movie as he can.* Even bad press would increase ticket sales. And he'd never liked her, so she would be the obvious target of his plan. Her attention snapped back to the moment at hand.

"No-o-o," Dreising said slowly. "I haven't heard a thing from the police." He paused. "What exactly is this person doing to you, Christina?"

"I found a message on my answering machine, then there were a couple of notes saying something terrible would happen to me." The latex pulled at her face now that it had dried. Talking hurt. "If I get any more messages I'm supposed to save them for the police and call right away."

Kurt suddenly came alive. He shook the wave off his forehead and bragged, "I get crank mail all the time—tons of it. Just trash the stuff."

"I did at first," she said. "But now I'm scared."

Dreising frowned. "I agree with Kurt. This is probably nothing more than someone's sick sense of humor. You can't let it ruin your performance."

"It won't," she promised. "But—well, is it all right if Steve stays around today?"

"I promise not to get in the way," he said quickly. "Chris might feel a little better if I'm here."

Dreising shot a doubtful glance at Kurt, then turned back to Christina. "I don't like groupies hanging around while we're filming."

Christina slipped her arm around Steve's waist and rested her head on his shoulder. "Please," she pleaded. "I'd feel so much safer with Steve here. I don't think I'll be able to concentrate on my scenes if he leaves."

Kurt lifted his eyes to the treetops and groaned, "Give me a break."

"I've got a rotten feeling in my gut about this," Dreising grumbled. "All right. He can stay." As he turned to leave, he pointed a warning finger at Steve. "You—don't get underfoot!"

"Yes, sir. Definitely not, sir," Steve called after the director as he strode away across the lot.

"So-o-o," Kurt drawled, sticking his thumbs in his belt loops exactly as he had done when he'd played the Carson Kid. "How long have you two been sweethearts?"

Christina wondered if Kurt always played roles, if he even knew when he was in character and when he was himself.

Steve shrugged. "We've been dating for over a year now. Right, angel lips?"

Christina was taken by surprise. He had to squeeze an answer out of her.

"Yeah, right. Just about a year." Observing the twinkle in Steve's eyes, she had to choke back the giggle working its way into her throat. She suddenly felt equally mischievous. "In fact, our anniversary is coming up this weekend. I'm sure Steve has bought me something terribly expensive. He spoils me."

Kurt lost his Texas twang. "He does?"

She nodded, grinning up at Steve, who was beginning to look worried. "In fact, he brings me little presents all the time. Do you have something for me today?" She stuck her hands into his pockets and tickled him.

"Hey, cut it out!" he gasped. "Get out of there!"

Kurt groaned and turned away. "You two just about make me puke."

Sitting in the makeup chair for three hours while Gus uglied her up was bad enough. Getting buried promised to be even less fun.

As soon as the crew finished setting up in the field below the castle's garden, Dreising pointed to a long wooden box with a gruesomely familiar shape and said to Christina, "Get in."

"In?" she croaked.

For some reason she'd imagined most of the scene shot around a closed coffin. The funeral guests would surround it while the actor who played the priest pronounced a few comforting lines. Then they'd take close-ups of her against a red velvet backdrop to make it look as if she were in the coffin. Apparently, she was wrong.

With a tight feeling in her chest, she obediently climbed into the box. Enough flowers surrounded it to bury the population of her hometown.

"Now," Dreising rumbled low in his throat, "you are dead, Chris. Don't move until I tell you. Don't as much as quiver an eyelash. Got that?"

"Yes," she said. It sounded easy enough.

He arranged her dress, her hair around her face the way he wanted it, then folded her hands one on top of the other across her chest. When he was satisfied, he stood back and yanked the Washington Redskins cap he was wearing down over his forehead.

"Kurt, stand here. That's it. All right. You're grieving for your child bride—the girl who meant the world to you . . . the young woman you'd planned to be with all of your life."

"Not exactly type-casting," someone in the crew muttered.

Christina stifled a laugh.

"She was your dream girl. Now she's dead," Dreising continued emotionally. "You'd do anything to bring her back. Anything! Got that?"

"Yes, sir," Kurt ground out.

Christina took shallow breaths to keep her chest from rising and falling. Soon the cameras would roll. Keeping still would be crucial.

"Places!" cried Amanda.

Christina sensed someone leaning over her, but she obeyed Dreising's order and clamped her eyes shut.

"So long, sweetheart," a breathy voice whispered.

Her eyes popped open but all she saw was a ring of faces encircling her coffin, staring mournfully down at her. The funeral party.

"I told you to keep those eyes *closed!*" Dreising barked.

She squeezed her lids shut again. Who had whispered those chilling words? She didn't have time to dwell on it. Suddenly, too much was happening.

"Roll cameras . . . and . . . action!"

Christina knew that by the time a real casket was brought to a grave site, it would already be closed. But Dreising had chosen this scene for a last tearful farewell from the young medical student to his beloved.

The priest delivered his valediction. Then she heard him step back from the grave. There was a muffled shuffling of feet as mourners turned away to leave. Recalling the script, Christina knew that Kurt would be moving closer to the coffin, grief ravaging his handsome young face. She sensed him bending over her. Something soft brushed her fingertips. The smell of a rose wafted to her nostrils. He was laying a single blossom on her breast. This was a little different from the way the script read, but it seemed a nice touch.

"I love you," he choked out. "I'll always love you, darling."

His voice was convincingly filled with suffering. It was all she could do to stop herself from reaching out to comfort him.

Then the coffin lid creaked as it lowered over her face, gradually closing out even the traces of gray light penetrating her eyelids . . . until darkness enclosed her.

Knowing neither Dreising nor the camera could see her, Christina at last opened her eyes. She could see nothing at all. Velvet brushed her nose when she tried to turn her head to loosen the stiff muscles in her neck. The pillowy fabric crushed her arms, pinning them to her chest. There might have been a few square inches of airspace, but not much more.

As the seconds ticked past and no one raised the coffin lid, Christina's heart raced. Her breath came in short anxious gasps. The air tasted thick on her tongue and clogged her throat.

One thousand . . . two thousand . . . three thousand, she silently counted off the seconds, straining to get a grip on her rising panic. She had been sure Dreising would shout, "Cut," throw open the coffin, and release her before continuing with the rest of the scene. Apparently Kurt's performance was so good the director allowed the cameras to roll during Kurt's next bit of dialogue with the priest.

Then she felt the coffin start to lower into the grave.

Her lungs worked, but seemed unable to pull in enough air. Sweat trickled down her forehead, and she felt suddenly dizzy. Still, she didn't dare call out for fear of interrupting the scene.

How long was Dreising going to keep this up? She remembered rereading the script last night:

Coffin lowers into the grave while Marty stands over it, crying silently. Close-up of coffin lid. Shovelful of dirt lands on—

Thud! Thud! Thump! Something was falling on the lid. They were burying her . . . burying her alive!

"Let me out!" Christina screamed. "Please! Let me out of here!"

But no one seemed to hear her cries. One after another, heavy clods of dirt fell, burying her deeper and deeper.

Chapter 7

Steve stood behind the cameras and lights in the field, watching the morbid scene being played out.

Christina's makeup had been ghoulish enough when they'd stood around talking, but once she'd climbed into the coffin with the flowers and mourners surrounding her, she looked . . . Well, there was no nice way of putting it, she looked like a three-day dead flounder, except worse. Because she was so special to him.

He felt as if he'd been slammed to the wrestling mat—unable to move, disoriented, gasping for air. In spite of understanding that what he was watching was all a game, a lump grew in his throat and his eyes blurred as the mahogany cover closed over Christina's ravaged face.

It was as if he truly believed he'd never see her alive again. His chest hurt almost as badly as when he'd cracked a rib at one of the meets last year. No . . . worse. Doc Cutler had taped him up, and he was as good as new in a couple of weeks.

There was no cure for death.

Steve shifted his feet restlessly as Kurt delivered his tender farewell over the grave. Although Steve expected the camera to stop then, Kurt and the minister continued their lines. The young star seemed to be on a roll. Dreising let him run with the rest of the scene.

Steve's glance drifted back to the coffin. Two stringy fellows in black overalls heaved huge shovelfuls of dirt into the grave as Kurt and the other actors moved a few steps across the meadow, the cameras following them while keeping the casket in the background.

Christina must be getting pretty antsy by now, he thought. Being shut in a coffin for a few seconds was one thing, but a good five minutes must have passed by now. Maybe more.

"I guess they drilled air holes in that thing," he whispered nervously to John Washington, who happened to be standing nearby.

John's eyes were riveted on the coffin, and he scowled as if thinking hard. "I don't remember seeing anyone working on it," he said slowly.

Steve felt as if a giant fist pounded him in the gut from the inside. His mouth suddenly went as dry as dust. Staring at the coffin lid, he thought he saw it move. But he couldn't be sure.

The grave diggers tossed on another load of dirt. A clod jumped off the lid, as if of its own will. Then, above the dull rattle of pebbles and earth on the wooden box, a soft cry was barely audible behind Kurt's emotional speech to the priest.

Steve shot a desperate look at Dreising. The director seemed totally wrapped up in his star's performance. He hadn't heard her!

Trying to catch the man's attention, Steve frantically waved both hands over his head. Dreising glanced his way once, shot him an irritated look, then intentionally ignored him.

Unable to wait any longer, Steve knocked aside one cameraman and dashed through the tall grass toward the coffin.

"Let her out!" he yelled. "She can't breathe!"

The actors fell silent. The crew and cast stared at Steve as if he were insane.

Clenching his teeth, Dreising let out a roar. "I told you to stay the hell out of my way!" Throbbing blue veins stood out on his temples beneath his baseball cap.

"Security!" barked Amanda Perry into her walkie-talkie.

"You don't understand!" Steve shouted, dodging between grips, who tried unsuccessfully to grab him. "Chris has been in there too long! Get her out!"

Two men in tan uniforms broke through the crowd.

"Stop him!" Amanda ordered, pointing at him.

Coming at him from opposite sides, the security guards seized him by the arms. He struggled briefly, dislodging one with a simple wrestling move, then quickly kicking the other guy's legs out from under him.

Gasping for air, Steve threw himself on the coffin and pried at the cover with his fingers.

The guards staggered to their feet and lurched for him.

"Never mind," Dreising groaned. "He's ruined the bloody scene anyway. Get the girl out of there."

Before the guards could reach the coffin, Steve shoved up the heavy lid.

As soon as he saw Chris's face he knew he'd done the right thing. Her makeup was smeared with sweat and tears. Her hands shook violently as she reached up toward him. He lifted her gently out of the wooden box.

"You all right?" he asked.

Blinking up at him, she drew a ragged breath. Fresh air rasped in and out of her hungry lungs. "I . . . I . . . oh, Steve. Awful . . . couldn't breathe."

She was trembling in his arms as he carried her to a spot beneath an elm tree where the grass had been trampled smooth by heavy equipment.

Kurt rushed over, closely followed by Dreising.

"Jerk!" Kurt spat. "Who do you think you are, crashing my scene?"

"Shut up." Dreising pushed the young actor aside and stared in disbelief at Christina, as if for the first time realizing that something had gone terribly wrong. "What happened?" he asked her. "All you had to do was relax and let Kurt finish his scene."

Christina felt dizzy and nauseous. She had to hold onto Steve just to sit up. "No air . . . couldn't breathe," she managed.

Dreising swung around. "Mitch!" he bellowed. "I told you to make sure there was a vent cut beneath the head of that box!"

"I did." The chief grip stared at Christina, obviously terrified that he'd be blamed for almost killing the costar. "I mean, I told Jack to get one of his boys to take care of it."

But his assistant Jack couldn't seem to remember which of his helpers had been given the responsibility of drilling the holes, and no one owned up to being assigned the job.

Dreising flew into a rage. "I should fire every one of you incompetent idiots!" he screamed, his face flaming red.

At last Christina caught her breath and the world slowed to a kinder spin. "I'm all right," she murmured weakly. "Please, it's no one's fault. Just an accident."

Dreising bent over her, his expression sincere and fatherly. "Sure you're okay, sweetheart?"

A chill zinged up her spine. She stared in horror at him.

Sweetheart! That was what the writer of that horrible note had called her. That was also the last word she heard before the coffin lid closed over her face. Had it been Dreising bidding her a sinister farewell, expecting that she'd be buried alive?

"I'm fine," she said shortly.

She had no proof. None at all, just as before. Whoever stalked her—whether that was Dreising or someone else—was being very clever.

"I'll call for a doctor," the director offered.

"No," she grunted, pushing herself up onto her feet with the help of Steve's shoulder. She desperately wanted to get away from Dreising . . . away from everyone. As Steve had pointed out, she couldn't know who to trust anymore. All she wanted now was to be left alone to think. "I need to rest," she stated. "Can I go back to my trailer?"

"Of course. Amanda?" Dreising called for his assistant.

She immediately appeared at his side. "Here."

"Let's set up for Kurt's next scene in the castle. We can shoot around Chris until she feels able to rejoin us."

Amanda shot an irritated look at Christina, as if she thought the delay was her fault. "Good idea," she muttered.

By the time Christina reached her dressing trailer she was feeling a little stronger and her breathing had almost returned to normal.

Steve insisted on accompanying her. She felt enormously grateful to him.

"Thanks," she said softly, as she stopped before opening the door.

He let out an embarrassed laugh. "Hey, no sweat."

"Really," she insisted. "You saved my life."

"I'm sure that at any minute someone in the crew would have realized you were in trouble and hauled you out."

"Maybe," she said doubtfully, then studied his solemn expression. "I can't figure out how you knew I was suffocating before anyone else."

"Call it intuition?"

"Jock intuition?" she teased.

He grinned. "Something like that."

She swung the door open and started inside, but sensed Steve wasn't following her. When she looked around to see why, he was still standing on the ground, staring at something across the lot.

She followed his gaze. The two security guards who'd tried to stop him earlier were approaching at a fast pace.

"What's the problem, fellas?" Steve asked tightly.

"Mr. Dreising wants you outta here," one of the men growled.

The other glowered at him dangerously, flexing his wide fingers as if they itched for a chance at a rematch.

"He gave me permission to stay and look after Miss English," Steve objected.

Christina slowly eased back down the steps, a hollow feeling filling her stomach. She didn't like the threatening way the men were sizing up Steve.

The talkative one of the two snorted. "Guess he changed his mind. He told us to kick your ass off location. Right now."

Steve stood his ground. Every muscle that showed below his T-shirt sleeve was as rigid as his voice. "What if I won't go?"

"I guess we'll have to throw you off," the guard snarled.

For a moment, the air felt as if it were charged with high-voltage electricity.

Christina was sure that if she didn't do something fast, she'd soon witness a bloody brawl. Although she sensed that Steve could take care of himself in most situations, she wasn't reassured by the odds—two against one.

"Steve, don't," she murmured, resting a hand lightly on his shoulder. "I'll be fine."

He glanced at her, then back at Dreising's thugs. "You sure?" he asked.

"Really. I'll be okay. I'll call you as soon as I get home tonight."

He nodded slowly. "Do that. And if you have any trouble at all, just call. I can be here in ten minutes."

Christina watched Steve stride across the lot, the two security men trailing after him. She felt a brief chill of fear, as subtle as a spring breeze. She was alone with strangers . . . strangers she couldn't trust . . . and one of those strangers preyed on her, used her, and tormented her for reasons she still didn't understand.

After locking herself in her trailer, Christina stripped off the latex foundation Gus had so carefully applied and scrubbed her face until it tingled and glowed. She lay down on the narrow cot and dozed off almost immediately. She napped fitfully, troubled by strange dreams of fanged monsters and dark caverns alive with slimy creatures. When she awoke her skin felt sticky with her own sweat.

Looking at the clock, she decided that she should head up to the castle. After all, the sooner the filming was completed, the sooner the madness would end.

As she walked across the lot, she scanned the clearing around the trailers. People rushed here and there, going about their work. At the far end of the lot she could see Amanda, weighed down by an armload of mail. John usually took mail duty, but he must have been running errands for Dreising this afternoon. Amanda had gotten stuck with the job again.

The woman stopped at each trailer, dropping off a few envelopes or a magazine. Christina decided to take her mail with her to read up at the castle between shots. She started toward her.

But Amanda didn't seem to see her, and when she stopped outside Christina's trailer, she scowled at the trailer door. Looking around slyly, as if she knew she was doing something wrong, she gingerly pried open the flap of a pink envelope.

That snoop! Kurt was right! She's really opening my mail! Christina thought, outraged, and started running toward her.

Amanda lifted the envelope flap. She hadn't even peeked inside when a jarring explosion shattered the air. It sounded to Christina exactly like a cherry bomb going off—the kind boys in her middle school used to throw on the sidewalk to make kids jump out of their skins.

Fierce, sharp, and eardrum shattering loud, it nearly knocked Christina off her feet.

When she regained her balance, Amanda Perry lay on the ground surrounded by a fluttering blizzard of paper. Where her face had been was now a mask of raw flesh. Bloody stumps were all that was left of her fingers.

Chapter 8

With a shriek of horror, Christina pushed her way through the shocked crowd toward Amanda. Strong arms intercepted her before she could reach the young woman, swinging her off her feet.

"You don't want to do that." It was John. His face was as white as her gossamer costume. "Doesn't look like you can help her."

"We just can't leave her like that!" sobbed Christina, hot tears streaming down her face.

People rushed about, shouting for help.

"It was a gunshot!" someone screamed. "I heard it."

Immediately, cast and crew started ducking into trailers, as if to get out of the line of fire. Beryl charged across the clearing, looking questioningly at her brother. She pulled up short when she saw Amanda lying on the ground.

"Oh, God!" she choked out. Her throat and jaw convulsed as if she were trying not to puke. She quickly turned her eyes away and staggered toward the nearest trailer. "I'll call . . . an ambulance."

John released Christina but kept a hand on her arm to make sure she wasn't going to try to get closer. One of the crew brought a blanket to cover Amanda. The man bent over and whispered something to her but she didn't answer, didn't move.

Dead. Good grief, she's dead! Christina's brain finally accepted the truth.

She felt totally helpless but, at the same time, seized by an impulse to do something—anything—as if she could still help Amanda. Stooping, she reached toward a few shreds of paper at her feet that had once been part of the envelopes Amanda carried.

As quickly as the thought occurred to her, another struck: *The police won't want anything touched. This is all evidence.*

She straightened quickly and looked at John. "A letter bomb," she murmured. "Someone rigged one of the envelopes she was carrying to explode."

John stared at her, his eyes darkly troubled. He swallowed twice before he was able to get out any words. "This is terrible." Like her, he seemed to be having trouble deciding what to do. "Come on, I'll walk you to your trailer. The ambulance and police will be here soon. They'll take care of Amanda."

Christina had never seen anyone die before.

A hollowness grew inside of her, and she found she couldn't move her feet for she was certain her knees would give way on her first step. She stared at the ground, working up her courage to walk away. Her blurred vision took in a dusty pink scrap of paper with charred edges.

Without thinking about what she was doing, she flipped it over with the toe of her sneaker. Although the scrap was less than an inch square, a few letters were visible on its singed surface. NA ENG.

And then she remembered. She remembered that it had been *her* mail that Amanda had been opening. She felt as if she'd been hit by a Mack truck doing eighty down Interstate 95.

"No!" Christina gasped, shaking John off. "I'll go alone!"

She bolted for her trailer, her throat filling with sour bile, the sky crashing down on her as she ran. The wind shifted, and Christina smelled something disgusting. A sickeningly sweet odor that reminded her of the biology lab at school one day when a couple of boys had roasted a dead mouse over a Bunsen burner. It smelt like burnt flesh. The stench of death.

Clapping her hand over her mouth, she vaulted up the steps and flung herself through the doorway. She was sick for a long time, but at last her stomach calmed down. She sat on the floor of the little bathroom, her head resting weakly on her arm against the edge of the toilet bowl, and she sobbed uncontrollably.

The police arrived two minutes before the ambulance. They were the same two officers who'd visited her home . . . who hadn't believed her when she'd told them the first time that someone was out to kill her.

Christina watched numbly from her window, knowing they would eventually come to her. They spoke with the security guards, then with Dreising. They spent some time squatting over Amanda's body, talking in low voices. They roped off the area, then started questioning people who'd hung around to watch the morbid ritual of a violent-crime investigation.

Christina curled up tight as a corkscrew on her couch, lifting the edge of the curtain only now and then to peer out at them.

Wiping a tear from her cheek, she told herself that she had to take control of her emotions. Soon the cops would start going from trailer to trailer. When they walked into her dressing room, she'd have to tell them she was sure that the bomb had been intended for her. If they didn't believe her this time, she didn't know what she'd do.

The worst part was, since they'd initially suspected she had rigged the other incidents as a publicity scam, they might blame her for Amanda's death, too.

See what happens when you try to be too clever, Miss English? she could hear the stocky lieutenant scolding her. *Someone gets hurt.*

She dropped her face into her hands and wished she'd never heard of Theodore Dreising or *Dark Memories*.

Randi Baxter jammed her foot on the brake just in time to avoid slamming into the tail end of the car she'd followed for two miles. She was cautious in all aspects of her life except one. Her dad claimed she had a lead foot. Her mom refused to ride with Randi when she drove.

She raised the heel of her hand to honk at the slowpoke sedan she'd followed all the way up the winding road toward the castle at the top of the hill, then noticed the car's official tags. State of Connecticut. She figured if she were behind an unmarked police car she'd better cool it.

Resigning herself to a snail's pace up the wooded hill, she let her mind drift elsewhere.

All week she'd been toying with the idea of visiting Christina on the set of *Dark Memories*. Her friend had invited her to drop by anytime. If Randi couldn't personally bask in the glory of starring in a movie herself—she might as well enjoy Christina's triumph. She didn't mind living vicariously.

Vicariously. Randi liked that word. It had an element of danger, yet it also meant that she was safe. Safe because whatever good or evil happened, it happened to someone else. She could simply stand by and watch.

Randi slowed at the guard shack, but no one seemed to be there, so she drove straight through behind the dark sedan. She parked the aging van that had been her older brother's.

The sedan pulled up alongside two blue Chevys. Only after she'd climbed out of the van did it click that they were police cruisers. A man and a woman started pulling what looked like suitcases out of the car she'd followed. A sticker on the windshield read FORENSICS.

Frowning warily, Randi started walking, following the sound of voices to a clearing in the trees just below the castle walls. A cluster of trailers sat among a field of ferns, looking like a family of gray whales floating in a green sea. She was still thinking about the police when she noticed the ambulance. She tightened up all over.

She'd only walked a few steps further before she spotted the blanket bunched up over an object on the ground. Her eyes slid along the rumpled plaid wool to one edge that had pulled up, revealing a sneakered foot. Dark crimson splotches stained the dirt all around.

Shoving a fist against her mouth, Randi stifled the scream rocketing through her throat. Her cheeks suddenly felt ice-cold, as if the blood had totally drained from them.

Panic seeped into her veins, burning through them like acid. *Chris! Oh, no!*

Randi broke into a blind run. She didn't know which trailer was Christina's. She read names over doors as she tore past one then another. But she couldn't find the right one, and she stopped in the middle of them, looking around, confused and terrified. What if she did find it and Christina wasn't there because she was underneath that—

"You looking for Chris?" a voice asked.

It was John Washington, Beryl's brother.

"Who is . . . *was* that?" she gasped.

"Dreising's personal assistant. You don't know her." John guided Randi away from the body and the forensic team that had followed her up the hill from the parking area.

Randi blinked, stunned. "What happened?"

"I'm not sure," John answered thoughtfully. "Christina seemed to think it was a letter bomb."

Randi felt sick. "It blew up in her hands?"

"Something sure did."

"Where's Chris?"

"In her trailer, I guess. She freaked out pretty bad. She was right here when it happened." He took a deep breath. "Her trailer is the one behind Kurt's. You can't miss his. It's the one with a star the size of an elephant."

Randi took off at a run in the direction John pointed. When she reached Christina's trailer, she pounded frantically on the metal door with both fists.

"Who is it?" a shaky voice called out.

"It's me, Randi!" She heard a latch click on the inside, and she rushed in, letting the metal door slam behind her.

Christina sat down on the edge of a narrow studio couch, her bare feet pressing into the floor, her eyes red and puffy.

Randi swallowed, then swallowed again, trying to catch her breath. "I saw her."

"It was supposed to be me," Christina groaned miserably.

"I . . . I thought about that as soon as I saw the body," Randi murmured, coming closer to her. "I was so scared it *was* you. But it isn't. And we don't know for sure it was meant for you."

Christina looked desolately up out of her hands. "*I* know. I have proof."

"Proof? What do you—"

Before Randi could finish, another knock sounded at the door. This time the caller didn't wait for an invitation.

Two policemen entered the little dressing room.

"I'm Lieutenant Draper with the Connecticut State Police, and this is Sergeant Mayhew, Miss English. We came out to your house a few nights ago."

"I remember," Christina said dully.

The lieutenant studied her. "In light of your earlier complaint," he began, "we'd like to speak with you about this incident."

A thick, black anger replaced Christina's fear. "Incident?" she gasped. "Is that what the police call it when someone's face gets blown off?"

Sergeant Mayhew shook his head solemnly. "It's not like that. We're taking this case very seriously. We overheard what you were saying to your friend as we approached the trailer. The walls are awful thin," he added apologetically.

She stared at him. "So now you know that I'm sure the bomb was meant for me."

"Why do you think this is related to the telephone threat and notes?" Draper asked gruffly. "You mentioned proof."

"The letters Amanda was carrying—"

"What about them?" the lieutenant interrupted.

"They were scattered, some blown into little pieces by the explosion. I started to pick a few of them up, but realized I shouldn't touch them."

"The one carrying the detonator and charge might have been burned up," the sergeant said, as if talking to himself.

"So?" Draper scowled at her impatiently.

Christina's throat felt as dry as a field of August straw. Her fear built as she voiced her theory. "On one of the scraps, only about this big—" She held up a thumb and finger an inch apart. "—there were five letters. N . . . A . . . E . . . N . . . G."

"Part of your name," Randi breathed.

"Last two letters of her first name and first three of the surname," Mayhew commented.

"Maybe," his boss muttered, unconvinced.

Christina shoved herself off the cot and stood toe-to-toe with the startled lieutenant. "How can you not believe me?" she shouted. "I don't *want* to be the person that letter was meant for. I'm not getting a kick out of any of this! And it's pretty obvious by now that I'm not imagining things!"

"It's all right. Calm down," the younger man said. He put a hand on her shoulder and backed her up to the cot until the mattress hit her calves and she was forced to sit. A kind smile showed beneath his red mustache. "We can't jump to conclusions. Understand? Now, think. Do you know of anyone who would want you dead?"

He reached for the stool in front of her dressing table, scooted it over in front of her, and straddled it. The lieutenant backed away and leaned against the door, saying nothing.

"I don't know," Christina said miserably.

"Where do you go to school? We'll start there."

"Hanover High."

"Know where it is?" the lieutenant asked the sergeant.

"Fifteen minutes from here," Mayhew said without taking his eyes from Christina's face. "Anything else?" he asked her.

"No," Christina murmured. "I might not be the most popular girl at school, but I'm not there enough to make enemies."

"Because of your acting jobs?" Mayhew asked.

She nodded, then glanced at Randi for support.

"Mostly the other kids are sort of . . . like in awe of Chris," Randi explained. "She's our school celebrity. No one hates her . . . I mean, well some of the girls might be a little jealous, but they'd have to be completely psycho to—"

The lieutenant cut her off. "We'll start at your school on the chance you've got a classmate with a mean streak."

"Meanwhile," Mayhew added, standing up, "your director has promised to beef up security on the lot." He reached over and patted her hand. "Try to relax. We'll get this crazy."

Christina didn't move until after they'd left, then she looked at Randi. "What do you think?"

"Sounds like they finally believe you. That's good."

97

"I guess." Christina sighed. "I just hope they find this maniac fast."

Lieutenant Draper and Sergeant Mayhew walked into Hanover High fifteen minutes after the dismissal bell rang and followed signs to the administration offices. The lieutenant handed Principal Ralph Hardy a search warrant.

A couple of hours later the two officers had thoroughly inspected both science labs and all eight hundred and fifty lockers lining the main corridors. They'd found nothing more deadly than a dozen packs of cigarettes, two lighters, and an arsenal of water pistols—all of which Hardy confiscated.

"Are there any other areas where students might store personal items?" the lieutenant asked Hardy.

"There are some lockers behind the gymnasium—in the boys' and girls' showers."

The two cops split up, one taking the boys' side, the other the girls'.

It didn't take long. Most of the lockers were empty and without padlocks. Students weren't supposed to leave personal items in the locker rooms overnight.

Mayhew cut the first lock in the boys' showers. Some kid had stashed a six-pack of beer. In the next he found a year's worth of *Playboy* magazines.

"Wouldn't want Mom to find these under your bed," he chuckled, replacing the magazines after he'd shaken them out and looked under the stack to make sure they didn't hide anything more sinister.

"I'm done," Draper called, joining him. "Nothing."

"This is the last one. Then we'd better start checking out the film crew."

Mayhew cracked the bolt cutters one more time. The broken combination lock clattered to the cement floor. The sergeant opened the locker. His eyes narrowed as he took in its contents.

"Bingo," he breathed.

Draper stepped forward, looking over the younger man's shoulder.

Every inch of the locker was plastered with photographs of Christina English—some torn from newspapers or magazines, others obviously candid shots snapped by an amateur. Here she was eating in the cafeteria. There, walking with an armload of books across campus.

The two men looked at each other.

Mayhew found his voice first. "Son of a gun if she wasn't right," he mumbled, balancing back on his heels. "This pervert's been stalking her."

The lieutenant looked stunned. "I honestly figured her for some hysterical teenager. If we'd listened to her—"

"Forget it," Mayhew said, thinking the same thing: Amanda Perry might be alive if they'd followed up on Christina's first complaint. "Let's find this kid before he kills again."

"First we have to find out who this locker belongs to," Draper pointed out.

"That shouldn't be too hard." The sergeant picked up one of the wrestling shoes. On its side was a patch with Hanover High's mascot—a coiled snake. He peered inside and read out loud, "S. Jackson."

They looked at each other.

"Let's go," Draper said.

Chapter 9

Steve climbed into the Pinto, started up, and gunned the engine out of the parking lot. Glancing in the rearview mirror, he saw Dreising's security goons watching to make sure he didn't turn back.

"Great! Just great!" He slammed the steering column with the heel of his hand. He wanted to be with Christina. She *needed* him. But now there was no way. He'd only get her into trouble if he tried to sneak back on location.

The confrontation with the guards left him feeling restless, ready for a fight. He was too wired to go home and study or watch TV, but couldn't come up with anything else to do. He just drove . . . drove further . . . drove further still, thinking of Christina, wondering if she was beginning to like him as much as he liked her.

The next thing he knew, he was staring at the sign on the interstate announcing the New Haven exit. He took it and got right back on the highway, this time heading north. Now what?

Forty-five minutes later he found himself sitting in the school parking lot and decided he might as well work out. It was the only way he knew to beat the tension knotting every muscle in his body.

In the locker room, he changed into shorts and a

T-shirt, then ran twelve laps around the cinder track. Three miles. Sweaty and high from an adrenaline rush, he strode back into the school. Some kids on the student council special-events committee were decorating the gym.

Not wanting to stop and chat, he slipped past without anyone seeing him and down the corridor to the weight room, which was tucked away behind the main gym. The small, mirrored room was used by the football and wrestling teams, and the weight-training class. Most students didn't even know the room existed.

Since his legs were already warmed up from running, Steve started with lower-body exercises. One Nautilus machine worked abductor and adductor muscles—inner and outer thighs. Next he moved on to leg curls and calf stretches. He finished off his leg workout with two sets of squats, supporting a barbell loaded with 150 pounds of metal plates on his shoulders.

Steve was changing the weights on the bench-press bar to start his chest and shoulder exercises when he heard voices in the locker room next door. Curious, he walked across the padded floor and cracked open the door.

Two cops were snapping locks off with a bolt cutter. At first he assumed they were looking for drugs or booze, and he wondered who'd be dumb enough to stash anything on school property. If the police found stuff, it would mean immediate suspension, or worse.

Then he realized that the cops meant to open *every* locker . . . including his.

Cold fingers of fear seized him by the throat. They'd find Christina's pictures! His mind clicked into gear. If these guys were investigating those crazy notes . . . well, it didn't take a genius to figure out what they'd think when they got a load of his photo collection.

Steve didn't wait for them to reach his locker. He grabbed his towel and raced out of the weight room, avoiding the students in the gym again by circling behind the volleyball nets and slipping out the side entrance to the parking lot. It had started to rain.

At his car door, he fumbled with the key three times before successfully sticking it into the lock. He heard a car screech into the lot, heading his way. Glancing up, he recognized a guy from the wrestling team behind the wheel. Four other kids were in the car with him.

"Not now!" he muttered, throwing himself into the driver's seat of the Pinto, in a rush to get away before the cops came out.

But the car pulled up alongside.

"Hey, Doomsday! Did ya hear?"

"Hear what?" he asked, cranking up the engine.

" 'Bout the girl that got killed up at the state park."

Steve froze, his hand still on the key in the ignition. His heart jumped into his throat.

"Killed?" He heard a voice that sounded distant but could only have been his own. "Who?" he demanded. "*Who* was killed, Kennedy?"

"No one knows," a girl with hair clipped back in a huge blue butterfly clip called from the backseat. "We were just up there, but like the place is crawling with cops. They won't let anyone near."

Steve blinked . . . blinked again, slumping in the torn vinyl seat. *Christina . . . oh God, not Christina!*

"Man!" a boy in the car gasped. "Look at that. The cops are here, too!"

Shocked back to reality, Steve slammed the Pinto's door shut and drove off blindly through the rain. Although he felt like flooring it, he forced himself to stay under the speed limit. He couldn't afford to attract attention to himself. If anything had happened to Chris, he didn't know what he'd do. But he did know one thing for sure . . . he was in worse trouble than he'd guessed.

Christina sat beside her father on the couch in her parents' living room, staring numbly at the Oriental carpet. The swirls of rich red wool under her feet reminded her of blood. Blood that had oozed from Amanda's ravaged face.

How could anyone do that to another human being? But that thought was quickly followed by another, just as disturbing. *How could I have been so wrong about Steve?*

Slowly the police officers' words had sunk in, searing her heart as if each one were a drop of acid. The most frightening part of this madness was—she'd really, really liked Steve. Because she'd always believed she was an excellent judge of character, she hadn't questioned her feelings when she'd spotted his photo in the yearbook. He looked interesting in a nice sort of way.

And the more she'd gotten to know him, the more comfortable she'd felt around him. He might be a jock, but he was smart and gentle, and he made her feel safe.

Safe! What a laugh! He was the one person she should never have trusted.

"Are you sure the locker is his?" she asked weakly.

"There's no doubt about it," Lieutenant Draper said, his eyes unrelenting. "Jackson's wrestling shoes were in it. Your principal telephoned his coach, who verified the boy often left equipment overnight, even though it was against school policy."

"I guess no one tells a wrestling champ he can't leave a towel and extra pair of shoes behind," Mayhew murmured.

Christina gazed blankly at the two policemen. "But he was s-s-so nice . . ."

"Some of the most brutal killers in history have fooled their victims and everyone in their communities for years," Mayhew said kindly. "Don't blame yourself for not seeing through him."

Her father coughed and laid a warm hand on Christina's, clenched on the sofa cushion between

103

them. "Chris's mother is out of town on business. I'd better call her before she reads about this in the papers. I don't want her thinking Chris was hurt. You do have everything under control now?"

"We're working it out, sir. We'll make sure your daughter is safe."

As Mr. English stood up, he gave the older officer a long serious look. "Lieutenant, you said that the same person sent the messages and planted the bomb. Are you absolutely sure?"

"We don't have fingerprints on the letter scraps, if that's what you mean, sir," Draper replied. He scratched thoughtfully between the buttons of his uniform shirt. "But there are certain personality types who prey on public figures—like rock stars and actresses. They become obsessed with that person. In your line of work, you've undoubtedly heard about the type, sir. When they can't get their attention any other way, they try to control their victim with threats and violence."

Mayhew looked at Christina. " 'If I can't have her, no one can.' That sort of thing."

Christina shivered. She wrapped her arms around her ribs and held on hard. "I . . . I just don't think Steve would—"

"We asked around at the school," the sergeant broke in, leaning forward urgently. "There were a bunch of students decorating the gym for an awards ceremony tomorrow. A couple of them remembered Steve asking you out. You turned him down."

"I was busy. I had a job!" Christina choked out.

"Maybe he didn't see it that way."

Her father sat down on the couch again and put an arm around her. "A young woman shouldn't have to accept dates from perverts to protect herself."

"He's not a pervert, Dad!"

He observed her with concern. "If this Steve tries to contact you, tell me or the police immediately. Don't even think about meeting him."

She folded her hands in her lap and stared at them.

"Miss English," the younger officer said in a quiet voice. "Your father's right. This boy is dangerous. In fact, it would be best if you didn't go anywhere alone until we arrest him."

Christina shook her head sadly. She'd never felt more lost or confused. Nothing seemed to matter anymore.

"In the meantime, we'll assign a man to watch you, just in case he tries again. Understand?"

She nodded.

"If Steve calls or you spot him, tell your bodyguard right away."

Her body shook uncontrollably as she stared speechlessly at the kindly sergeant, fixing on his red mustache.

"We'll be in touch tomorrow morning," the lieutenant told her father. He turned back once more to Christina as he moved toward the door. "And don't open any mail. Let the officer on duty do that for you."

After her father had showed them out, he returned to the living room. Christina hadn't moved from her seat on the couch.

"Are you all right?" he asked.

She nodded. One silent lie wouldn't hurt if it made him feel better.

John Washington listened to his sister's end of the telephone conversation from the hallway outside her bedroom. He didn't normally eavesdrop, but this was a matter of life and death.

"Are you kidding?" Beryl gasped into the receiver. "No way!"

He peeked around the corner. She was sprawled across her bed, chomping on a wad of gum, gossiping on the phone with her best friend Margo as if nothing unusual had happened that day.

105

"Of course I didn't get a close look at her," Beryl exclaimed. "I mean, who would want to?"

She paused to listen again and blow on her wet fingernails. She'd painted them Rhapsody Red, her favorite color.

"Yeah, the cops were asking everyone tons of questions, but they spent the most time in Christina English's trailer. My guess is, they think she did it . . . or else they figure she was supposed to get the letter instead of that witch Amanda."

Beryl puffed on her nails one last time, then frowned at them as if dissatisfied with their vivid sheen. They looked to John like an animal's claws, dripping with blood.

Uncomfortable with that thought, he shifted his feet. The floorboards creaked, giving him away.

Beryl shrieked. "You snoop! What do you want?"

"Nothing . . . uh, I just came to borrow your math book." He crossed the room quickly, snatching the text off her desk. As soon as he was out of her room, he pressed his back against the hallway wall, waiting for the conversation to continue.

"Well, it doesn't bother me one way or the other," Beryl continued after a minute in a sly tone. "If Christina blew up Amanda Perry, the police will arrest her. On the other hand, if she gets knocked off by some psycho-killer . . . Gee! I guess that leaves her part in *Dark Memories* open." She giggled.

John couldn't tell if she was joking or serious.

These days, the more he thought about Beryl and the way she was, the more he worried about her.

You'd love to see Christina dead. Wouldn't you, dear sister? John thought grimly as he stalked back to his bedroom, the math book he hadn't really needed wedged under his arm. And his mother . . . she'd be positively overjoyed. He threw the book on his bed beside the stack of library books he should have returned that morning.

For a long time he stood at his window staring at the sunny yellow daffodils and red tulips lining the walk to their apartment.

Even though Christina was exhausted, she tossed in bed, unable to sleep. Moon shadows of tree branches outside her bedroom window waved eerily against her wall. She focused on the silhouettes, envisioning in them sinister creatures creeping up to her window, peering in at her while she slept. Trembling, she drew the sheet tighter over her Phantom of the Opera nightshirt and squeezed her eyes closed.

That didn't work.

She rolled over in bed, pulled the pillow over her head, concentrated on repeating her lines for a scene they'd do tomorrow.

To everyone's surprise, Dreising had refused to hold up shooting for even one day after Amanda's death. Instead, he'd announced that there would be five minutes of silence at noon—during lunch break.

"The only way to beat a lunatic is to ignore him," she'd overheard him boasting to a cluster of reporters who'd arrived just an hour after the bomb went off. "Amanda wouldn't have wanted us to quit. She was a professional to the end."

Christina tried not to think of Amanda, of blood on her mirror, or what might happen now that a murderer had killed the wrong person. But no amount of reasoning or blocking out reality helped.

At last she decided that the only way to convince herself no one lurked outside her window was to look. But what if she did and someone *was* there? What if Steve had somehow eluded the police and come after her?

A branch scraped the window screen. She flattened her hands over her ears. The branch scraped again, like fingernails across a chalkboard, chasing prickles up her spine.

At last she couldn't stand it another minute. She threw off the bed covers, planted her feet on the bare wooden floor, and tromped over to the window. *If I snap off that stupid branch,* she thought, *then maybe I can get some sleep.*

Even as her hands pulled back the creamy-white drapes, her brain spoke to her. *No branches reached the window last night. Something else is scratching at your screen. Don't open the window!*

But, as always, her reflexes lagged behind her thoughts. She'd yanked open the curtains and pushed up the window before it sunk in that a face *was on the other side of the screen!*

A boy's face . . . reflecting the light from her night-table lamp . . . eyes wide and staring . . . hair standing out wildly around his head.

Christina screamed, letting the curtains fall back in place. "Daddy, come here quick!"

Shaking from head to toe, she backpedaled toward her bedroom door. Her father didn't come, didn't answer.

He's in the study, she thought. Two floors below in the basement of their house. He couldn't hear her.

Run! Run! her brain screamed. All she had to do was make it out her front door onto the lawn. The cop sitting in the cruiser out front would see her. She'd be safe.

But, as if in a nightmare, she found it impossible to tear herself from the spot where she stood.

Then a strange thing happened.

As the seconds ticked by and no one ripped through the screen to grab her by the throat, her breathing slowed and her heart ceased racing.

Curiosity beckoned her forward, step by cautious step. Why hadn't he crashed through? Why hadn't he killed her by now? The only thing stopping him was a flimsy wire mesh. Gingerly, she lifted the heavy drapes and peeked out into the night.

The face was gone.

Taking a deep breath, Christina began to feel a little braver. She moved closer, trying to see past the grainy screen.

Enshrouded by the new leaves of the sturdy maple growing outside her bedroom window, Steve crouched in a crook of one giant limb in a posture of defeat. His knees were pulled up protectively against his wide chest, his head resting on them. Muscled arms curled around his legs as the wind whipped at his T-shirt. On its back a snake coiled around the letter W, for wrestling.

"Steve," she whispered.

He didn't move.

Christina glanced speculatively toward her bedroom door. She knew what she *should* do. Go straight downstairs to her father's study and tell him Steve was outside.

But a twinge of doubt haunted her. *What if Steve isn't the killer? You'll be setting up an innocent kid.*

On the other hand, if Steve was a murderer she'd be risking her life for some boy she hardly knew.

Christina swallowed and gazed out into the moonlight. He was still there, apparently unaware that she was watching him. He looked incredibly sad.

"Steve!" she hissed, keeping her voice low.

He leaned his head to one side, as if trying to identify a sound. When his glance settled on her window, he immediately sat up straight. A look of relief flooded his dark eyes.

"Stay there!" she whispered shakily. "Don't come any closer!"

"I just want to talk to you," he said, crawling toward her like a big cat on the wide limb.

"We'll talk," she promised quickly. "Just stay where you are."

Understanding dawned in his expression. "You think I was the one who sent those notes?"

"The police say it was you. They also think you rigged a letter bomb meant for me."

He looked shell-shocked. "The kids at school were right? Someone was killed today on the set?"

"Amanda, Dreising's assistant. She opened a letter bomb."

Steve clamped his lips shut and looked away.

"Well?" she asked.

"What do you want me to say?"

"That you didn't do it, of course!"

"I didn't!" he insisted in a hoarse whisper, glancing toward the street worriedly. He must have already spotted the cop, she thought. "But I don't know how I can prove it."

"Where did you go after the guards kicked you off the set?" she demanded.

"Driving around. I was steamed, but there was nothing I could do about it."

"Before you left, you didn't give Amanda a letter addressed to me?"

He bit his lip, shaking his head. "Chris, I'd never hurt you. Man, you've gotta believe me!"

She studied his earnest brown eyes. Was this all an act? If a script called for her to fake that oh-please-don't-think-nasty-things-about-me expression, she could have pulled it off easily. But she was a professional actress. Steve was into sports, where honest effort, physical strength, and lightning reflexes counted. He didn't look the type who'd find lying easy.

However, if the police were right, Steve was insane. People who were crazy could be ingeniously deceptive.

"I want to believe you," she admitted softly.

"Why don't you?" he asked, gazing at her through the screen with puppy-dog eyes.

"The police say you're . . . you're obsessed with me. They found all sorts of pictures in your locker and—"

Steve swore under his breath. "I never wanted you or anyone else to know about those. They were private . . . like a diary or a scrapbook."

"Why did you save them?"

He didn't answer for a long moment. It started to rain again. A chilly wind blew through the tree branches.

At last Steve murmured, "Because I love you."

For a full minute Christina couldn't draw a breath. Then she forced herself to gulp down a couple of lungfuls of air. It tasted like the night—moist and sweet, with the smell of the first grass cutting of the season.

"You don't even know me," she choked out.

"I've always known how talented you are. I've seen every one of your performances. And I knew you were beautiful. No one could miss that. But now I know that you're not a snob like some kids at school say."

He looked suddenly sheepish, as if afraid he'd hurt her feelings. But she'd long ago accepted the fact some students talked behind her back because they were jealous.

"I know you like me," he rushed on, "or you wouldn't be taking a chance by talking with me."

He was right. She did like him. A lot. But that didn't mean she was going to do anything dumb like ask him into her bedroom, even if it was raining and cold. Although . . . Steve did look terribly uncomfortable perched on that tree limb.

"Maybe I just don't like the idea of throwing someone into jail without proof he did anything wrong," she murmured.

He blinked at her and sat down on the limb, letting his long legs dangle on either side.

"Thanks for not blowing the whistle on me," he whispered. She guessed that he must be disappointed she hadn't at least said she liked him.

"What are you going to do now?" she asked.

"I don't know." He thought for a moment. "I guess I'd better chill for a while, stay out of sight."

"But you can't go home . . . or go to school or anywhere you usually hang out," she reasoned. "The police will be waiting for you."

"Yeah," he said slowly. "I guess I don't have any choice. Somehow I have to clear myself. The only way to do that is to find out who was behind those messages and the bomb." He started to turn away.

"Steve," she called softly.

"Yeah?"

"Be careful."

Chapter 10

Christina wriggled on top of the tall wooden stool.

"Hold still," Gus Murphy warned.

"That thing's cold!" she complained.

"I'll take it off in a minute. Just have to try it on for size this time."

Gus pressed a plastic pouch of fake blood against her chest, above the low neckline of her bathing suit. While he secured it loosely with surgical tape, Christina tried her best not to move. After the fiasco with the funeral scene, she dreaded today's shoot.

In the script, the two scenes they'd be doing today actually came before the funeral. But directors rarely filmed stories in the order they were written. Many factors, including weather and the availability of talent, dictated the order of shooting.

"How hard will Sir Neville have to ... you know ... stab me to make me bleed?" she asked.

"Not hard at all, love," Gus assured her. "Fact is, the knife will look plenty sharp, but it has a retractable blade and just enough of a jagged edge to puncture this plastic. To anyone watching the film, it will look as if he plunged that blade straight into your heart."

"Super," Christina muttered.

She let her mind drift off as Gus continued working on

her, adjusting the little sack at different angles. She was still worried about Steve. During a lousy night's sleep, she'd changed her mind a dozen times about telling the police he'd visited her. In the end, she'd decided she owed him at least a couple of days' silence while he tried to prove he had nothing to do with Amanda's death. He'd rescued her from the coffin, hadn't he?

"There!" Gus exclaimed, at last pulling the tape and pouch off. "I think that'll work fine. You'd better hightail it over to the castle. Ted is waiting." He wiped his hands on a damp towel, shaking his head. "Been in a foul mood since yesterday, he has. Poor Amanda. The little bird never knew what hit her."

Christina looked at Gus. "Aren't you surprised that he's going on with the film? I mean, he didn't even close down for one day after her death."

Gus rearranged pots of makeup on a shelf. "Naw. If you knew Ted like I do, you'd understand, love. He's all business. Nothin' gets in his way. Nothin' and nobody."

Christina thought about Dreising as she dashed across the lot toward the castle. In spite of what Gus had said, it seemed to her that the director was taking his assistant's death awfully well.

Pulling a blouse over her bathing suit, she looked around anxiously as she wove between trailers and equipment toward the castle. It didn't take her long to spot the police officer who'd been assigned to watch her.

He was dressed like one of the crew, in T-shirt and jeans, probably to make himself less conspicuous. Earlier that morning, he'd followed her from her house in an unmarked car. Apparently he or one of his buddies had sat outside all night, but they hadn't seen Steve.

Steve, she mused. Why did she so desperately want to believe he was innocent?

"Hi!" a voice called out unexpectedly.

She spun around. "John! You scared me. How's the

114

job going?" She was actually glad to have some company to chase away her dark thoughts.

"No complaints. I'm always busy." He cheerfully held up a jar of green slime. "Goop to spread on the castle walls for your big bug scene."

She wrinkled her nose. "I don't even want to think about it," she groaned.

John laughed. "I remember how much you always hated spiders." He paused. "After this scene, you do the stabbing. Right?"

"Yeah," she admitted dully.

John looked around, as if concerned that someone might be listening to them. His glance lingered on the plainclothes cop, who was standing just out of hearing range but watching them closely.

"There are a lot of rumors around the set," he whispered.

"About what?"

"They say that bomb was meant for you."

She attempted a casual shrug, but couldn't hide the tension in her voice. "The police seem to think so."

John opened his mouth, then hesitated.

"What is it?" she asked.

"I . . . I'm not sure."

She followed his wandering glance to the balcony on the castle's turret, looming above them. A chunk of mortar fell away and landed on the flagstone patio, smashing into powder on impact. The area beneath the balcony had been roped off for the safety of crew and cast. The old place seemed to be falling apart, losing a chunk here, a piece there several times a day.

John turned back to her. "This may sound weird to you, but—well, you know that I really like you, Chris. I always have."

She smiled at him, then touched his arm affectionately as she started walking again. "I know. I like you too."

John steered her around the roped patio. "After all, we

115

were like . . . boyfriend and girlfriend for a long time."

Not so long. For two months, Christina thought. But to John that might seem like quite a while. She didn't correct him.

"And," he continued in a quiet voice, "I still feel sort of . . . sort of responsible for you."

"That's sweet. But the police are looking out for me," she reassured him.

"Yeah. The thing is, they don't know you or the people around you like I do. They can't possibly protect you twenty-four hours a day."

"The police had a stakeout outside my house all night."

"And you have a shadow today," he observed, scowling at the plainclothes man, who scowled back at him. Christina knew all she had to do was wave and the cop would be at her side in a flash. "I just mean—well, even the police make mistakes. If someone's seriously out to get you, they'll find a way."

Christina jerked to a stop and stared at John, her chin quivering. "Stop it. You're scaring me."

"I'm sorry. It's just that I'm really worried that—" He broke off, his eyes locking on some point across the set.

Christina followed his glance, but all she saw was a busy swarm of extras and technicians.

Then what he was trying to say suddenly hit home. Her breath caught in her throat, and the blood in her veins ran cold with horror.

"You know something, don't you?" she accused. "Someone right here on the set is doing this to me!"

John ran his tongue over dry lips. "I didn't say that," he said quickly. "I'm just worried about you. The smart thing to do is quit the film, get yourself out of the lime-light. Whoever this . . . this person is will lose interest in you."

"Leave the film?" she repeated in disbelief.

He seized her hands and squeezed them, his grip damp with perspiration. "Listen, making a movie isn't worth losing your life," he argued.

Christina glared at him. "*Who is it?* John, you have to tell me."

She sensed the cop moving closer to them, apprehension growing on his face.

"I . . . I can't," John stammered. Releasing her, he backed away quickly. "I don't know. Honest. Just drop the film before it's too late."

She stared after him as he trotted through the yawning portal of the castle, Gus's homemade slime in one hand.

"You okay, Miss English?" her bodyguard asked from close beside her. "I figured he was just one of your friends."

"He is. I'm fine," she murmured dully.

But Christina couldn't lose the sinking feeling in her stomach that, despite John's denial, he knew the identity of Amanda's killer. And if he refused to tell her, it could only be because he was protecting that person. As far as she knew, there were only two people in the world John cared about that much—his mother and Beryl.

Inside the castle nothing looked like a real castle should. In place of torches or candles, high-intensity electric beams ran off of a generator, brightening the interior of the grand hall to a summer day's glare. A modern refrigerator stood off-camera, chilling soda and bottled water for the thirsty cast. Electric cables snaked across the stone floor and soared upwards through the dank air toward the rafters, creating an obstacle course for anyone crossing the room.

A few square yards of floor at one end of the room had been cleared of equipment. Here the scenery crew had constructed a passageway. They'd matched Styrofoam stones to the real rocks in the castle walls, building a

117

short tunnel through which Christina would crawl. By altering camera angles and repeatedly shooting sections of the same space through a cutaway side, an illusion of a very long passageway would be created.

Christina watched regretfully as the bug man and his helpers released boxes of beetles and spiders into the tunnel.

A hand settled on her shoulder, and she automatically tensed.

"Are you ready?" Dreising asked.

She looked up at him warily. John really liked working for the director. How far, she wondered, would a young production assistant go to protect his boss and keep his job? Could John be protecting Dreising instead of his mother or sister? A veteran FX man would certainly know about things like explosives.

"I suppose," she said tightly. "Let's just do this fast."

"No," the director corrected her. "Let's do it good." He patted her on the back. "Remember, Chris, in this scene your new husband is missing. You wake up and find he isn't in bed, so you're looking for him. You already know this resort isn't what either of you'd expected. It's spooky, feels haunted—and it is. Sir Neville is watching you."

"So—I set out to look for Kurt and when I find this gross tunnel positively swarming with insects, I dive right in?" she asked sarcastically.

He frowned at her, his eyes dangerously dark. "Forget about logic, sweetheart. Teenage girls in movies aren't big in the brains department."

Christina glared at him, offended.

But he was already striding across the set to consult with his camera crew.

It took only ten minutes for the first few shots. Thankfully, Christina didn't have to touch any bugs. She just contorted her face into all sorts of horrified expressions while the cameras whirred softly, taking their close-ups. After that, things got outright gross.

The bug man and his assistant placed bottle-cap–size beetles, writhing millipedes, and fat hairy spiders at strategic spots all over her hair and shoulders. Closing her eyes, she tried to envision something pleasant and extremely far away from the crumbling old castle.

She imagined she was back on the beach at Cannes in France where she'd modeled for a swimsuit photo spread in *Seventeen*. She could almost taste the syrupy bubbles as she sipped a tall, frosty glass of Orangina soda. Stretched out beside her on a soft, white towel in the sand was a young man with a muscled back and broad shoulders.

He lay face-down so that she couldn't see his features. Christina screwed her glass down into the hot sand and spread suntan oil on his shoulder blades and wide neck. Lazily, he rolled over and smiled at her.

It was Steve.

Feeling blissfully warm and happy, she smiled down at him. "Want a sip of my soda?" she asked.

But when Steve opened his mouth to speak, he snarled like a wild animal and lashed out at her with long claws.

"No!" she cried, her eyes flying open.

"Hold still! You'll knock off the beetles!" the bug man shouted.

Christina gripped a fake rock and willed herself not to move again. What did the terrifying daydream mean? That Steve was not the boy she thought he was? That he was every bit as dangerous as the police claimed?

But it was hard to keep her mind on unraveling a mystery while two guys were decorating her with bugs. Now she knew how Kate Capshaw must have felt in that *Indiana Jones* movie.

"Geez, I hate this," she muttered.

The bug man grinned. "Think how my poor little pets feel about gigantic you. Now don't move suddenly. If you knock any of these beauties off, you'll squish them

119

when you start crawling into the tunnel. The really big ones are expensive. Had to fly them in from South America." he explained proudly.

"I'll try to be careful," she promised dryly.

The scene required five takes, but Dreising finally seemed satisfied.

"Cut!" he shouted. "Break for one hour. The stabbing scene's after lunch."

"Lunch," Christina grumbled, as the bug man rushed up to retrieve his precious pets. She'd lost her appetite hours ago.

Chapter 11

Everything that could possibly go wrong went wrong that afternoon.

First, one of the cameras had to be replaced. Then there was a power failure, and additional generators needed to be hauled up the hillside. The antique wiring in the old castle apparently couldn't support the crew's modern equipment. Delays ate up time and meant that several scenes had to be rescheduled for another time when full power was restored. It was eight-thirty that night, and raining harder than it had the night before, when Dreising finally dismissed his cast and crew.

Exhausted and hungry enough to eat a steak the size of a small car, Christina dragged herself back to her trailer. The man who'd replaced her daytime bodyguard followed close behind.

"I'll be just a minute. I have to wash up and change clothes," she explained.

"Take your time," he told her. "I've got all night."

He waited outside while Christina went in and ran water in the tiny shower stall. She peeled off her clothing and, still in her bathing suit, ducked into the steaming spray. Closing her eyes, she turned her face up into the hot prickles of water.

The stabbing scene was one of those that had to be delayed until the end of the day's work. It had been almost too real.

Of course, she knew the actor who played the dead Sir Neville. He was a veteran of dozens of horror films—totally believable as a bloodthirsty werewolf, zombie, swamp fiend, or alien creature—but a sweet, gentle man when he was out of costume. However, it was easy to get carried away by Gus's awful special effects. When Sir Neville's dagger had plunged into the plastic sack taped above her breasts, her scream vibrated with honest terror.

Christina sighed, feeling the tension ease out of her muscles as the hot water worked its magic. The fake blood on her chest washed slowly down the drain in ruddy swirls. She thought of Hitchcock's famous shower scene in *Psycho*, and shivered.

Quickly stepping out of her bathing suit, she rinsed it thoroughly and squeezed out the last crimson traces until the water ran clear. After hanging the dripping suit over the shower-curtain rod, she reached for the towel she'd left folded on the toilet seat.

It wasn't there!

Christina yanked back her hand and clapped it over her mouth to stifle the scream bursting from her throat.

Trembling, she stood in the shower stall counting her heart beats, wondering if the next would be her last.

A hand thrust a bunch of damp pink terry cloth through the opening between the curtain and tiled wall. With a muffled whimper, she seized the towel and wrapped it quickly around her.

"Don't panic," a familiar voice whispered. "It's just me . . . Steve. Sorry, I had to borrow your towel."

Not knowing whether to feel grateful or scream her guts out, Christina squeezed her eyes shut and said a silent prayer. *Please get me out of this!*

"I'll wait in the other room. Just don't call the cop," Steve pleaded. "I have to talk to you."

As soon as she heard the bathroom door click shut, Christina leaped out of the shower and locked the door behind him. Gasping for breath, her head whirling in confusion, she leaned against the sweaty tile.

If she called for her bodyguard, he might crash into the trailer with his gun drawn. What would he do when he saw Steve? Open fire, and ask questions later?

Although the police had only circumstantial evidence against Steve, that didn't mean they were wrong. Still, part of her refused to accept his guilt.

Hastily, she pulled on underwear, jeans, and a T-shirt she'd brought with her into the bathroom. She combed out her wet hair.

When she opened the bathroom door, Steve was sitting on the edge of her bed, staring intently at her. He looked as if he'd been running in the rain for the last hour. His hair was still wet and the shoulders of his jacket were a single soggy, dark splotch. When she made no move toward the outside door, a shadow of relief passed over his sad eyes.

"I know you're afraid of me." His voice was so low she could barely hear him. "Thanks for not giving me away . . . again."

She nodded stiffly. "It was stupid to come here. If the police catch you—"

"I had to show you this." He held up three short pieces of plastic-coated wiring. One green, one red, one black.

"So?" she asked, frowning.

"I found these beside the trash dumpster at the bottom of the parking area."

Christina studied them more closely. "They're just wires. There are all sorts of electrical cables and equipment on a movie set."

"Not this kind. See how thin these wires are? Almost like thread."

"Maybe Gus uses them."

"Your makeup man?"

"He's also our FX specialist for makeup and tricks that don't require a stunt person. Like today, he rigged me with a plastic pouch so that it would look as if I were bleeding when I was stabbed."

Steve stared thoughtfully at the wires. "I remember seeing some of those blood bags in his trailer along with masks, wigs, and a lot of other stuff. But I don't remember seeing any wires."

"He has little drawers full of all sorts of stuff," Christina said.

Steve looked unconvinced.

"Well, where do you think they came from?" she asked.

"My guess is, someone right here on location used wires just like these to make the letter bomb. That means that your crazed fan is a careful planner, and it's someone you know . . . someone working here on the set." He looked at her solemnly, waiting for a reaction.

"You all right in there, Miss English?" the cop called from the other side of the trailer door.

"Fine. I'm fine!" she yelled, reaching over to her dressing table for her hair dryer. She switched it on high. "Just drying my hair."

Her throat tightened as Steve's words sank in deeper. "I think you're right. It's someone right here. But we still don't know who . . . or why."

She took a deep breath, absentmindedly fluffing her long hair in the stream of heat. "Before Amanda was killed, I wondered about Dreising or Kurt pulling some publicity scam. *Dark Memories* is running on a tight budget. Rumor has it that the two million Kurt gets plus his percentage of the tickets sold will drain Dreising dry."

"Unless the film's a smash hit?"

"Right," she said.

Steve thought for a minute. "But it doesn't have to be one of them," he pointed out. "Does anyone who works on the film hold a grudge against you?"

She laughed. "Other than Kurt because I refused to go out with him? I don't even know most of these people."

"Some you do. Like the extras from school."

"Beryl, Stephanie, and Laura. And John is working as a production assistant."

Steve nodded meaningfully. "Do you think one of those girls or someone else—like one of Kurt's old costars—might want your part so bad she'd be willing to kill you for it?"

Christina started to shake her head automatically, then remembered John's odd behavior earlier that day. "Beryl and her mother would probably send up fireworks if I accidentally croaked," she murmured miserably. "But I can't believe either one of them would actually *do* anything to make that happen."

A loud pounding on the door cut her off. "Miss English, I'm supposed to take you straight home. Almost everyone's left. Your parents will be worried."

"Coming!" she called above the whine of the dryer. Then, in a hushed voice to Steve: "Those wires won't convince the police that someone in the production company rigged that bomb. They'll figure you planted them, or dropped them accidentally when Dreising had you thrown out."

"I guess," Steve said, looking desperate. "But I haven't come up with anything else." Reaching out, he shut off the dryer and stared at her seriously. "I need you to believe in me, Chris. I have no one else to turn to, nowhere to go. Let me stay in your trailer tonight. It's the last place they'll look. If anyone shows up, I'll catch them. If not, I promise I'll disappear before morning."

Christina weighed her options. She felt torn in too many directions. If she turned Steve away, the police would find him. If she trusted him, she might be signing her own death certificate.

Before she could say anything, he leaned forward and kissed her quickly on the lips. "I'd never hurt you," he whispered.

That did it.

"Okay," she agreed, her heart thudding in her chest. "Stay here. There's a tunafish sandwich, some milk and fruit in the refrigerator. But we'd better find out the truth fast. It's just a matter of time before the police catch up with you."

"Thanks." He smiled weakly at her. "You won't regret it."

I hope not, she thought.

Christina pulled her car into the driveway of her parents' house and sat behind the wheel. All the way home she'd felt as if someone were watching her. But that was ridiculous. She'd been going fifty miles an hour, and the only car behind her had been the unmarked police vehicle, which was there to protect her.

Forcing her fingers to unclench from around the steering wheel, she looked up at the comfortable white Cape Cod with green shutters.

The front porch light was on. Her father would be waiting up for her. In two more days, her mother would be home. The police finally believed her, and everyone was looking out for her safety. What possible reason did she have to be afraid?

But she was afraid. Deathly afraid, and she couldn't help it.

Sensing motion to her left, Christina turned her head to see someone peering at her through the driver's-side window. She jumped, letting out a faint yip of shock.

"You all right, Miss English?"

It was the police officer. This one was younger than the others, even younger than Mayhew, with hardly a shadow of a beard. But like the others, he wore a serious, watchful expression.

"Fine," she murmured. "I was just resting."

He opened the car door for her.

"You look as if something's wrong. Anything you need to tell me?"

She climbed out of the car, feeling more strongly than ever the sense that someone was observing them.

"I . . . I think that . . . I'd feel better if you were inside the house tonight," she finished quickly.

"Sure," the young cop agreed with a smile. "I'll be more comfortable on your dad's couch than out here in the car anyway. I'll call headquarters and let them know."

The figure crouched behind the dense hedge of mountain laurel that had grown beside the English family's house for more years than Christina had lived. His fingers slowly parted the tender green branches as his eyes glowed with secret anticipation, watching as Christina walked slowly into her house, casting a final worried look over her shoulder.

"Come on . . . come on . . ." An impatient hiss escaped his lips. "Tonight you die. Tonight's the night—oh, baby, oh." The chant began to sound like a pop song.

The state cop returned to his car. He was sure that the cop would settle down with a thermos of black coffee as he had the night before. In spite of a healthy dose of caffeine, he'd eventually drop off to sleep. The watcher itched to follow the girl now, not wait another second, but there must be no witnesses. Especially none toting a .45 automatic.

To his dismay, the cop didn't get into his car. Instead, he leaned in through the vehicle's window, spoke briefly over the radio, then strolled up the brick walk to the house. Humming, he casually let himself in through the front door.

Rage built inside the watcher's heaving breast. He felt as is if he'd explode.

"No. No. No!" He cursed violently.

Why hadn't he foreseen this happening? Now he'd have to wait one more night. Somehow Christina's watchdog would have to be eliminated, then he'd kill her.

Chapter 12

Christina dragged herself out of bed. Her head ached. Her mouth tasted like the inside of an old purse. And—worst of all—she could still feel little spider feet creeping all over her, even though she'd showered a second time before climbing into bed.

As she stared into the mirror at her bloodshot eyes, resenting the fact she had to go anywhere today, she heard voices rising from the first floor.

One voice definitely belonged to her cop. But the other definitely did not belong to her father, and he was supposed to be the only other person in the house with her.

Grabbing a pair of jeans and a sweatshirt from the pile of dirty laundry accumulating on the floor at the foot of her bed, Christina quickly dressed. She cautiously cracked open her bedroom door and peered down the hallway toward the stairs.

"No one goes up there without *my* say-so!" growled the cop. "You'll have to leave."

"But I'm her best friend! I practically *live* in this house!"

Christina's depression evaporated.

"Randi!" she cried. Nobody cheered her up faster, even in a crisis. "It's all right, Officer. She can come up."

Her friend took the stairs in threes. "Some goon you have down there. Thought he was going to gun me down when I let myself in the front door," she grumbled.

Christina giggled. "I forgot that you had a key." The Baxters and Englishes had swapped emergency keys years ago, in case someone got locked out. The two girls often used the keys to visit at odd hours when they didn't want to disturb sleeping parents.

"What's up?" Christina asked, shutting her door behind them.

Randi rolled her brown eyes dramatically. "Everyone at school is talking about how weird it is that Steve Jackson's trying to kill you. The police have the school under surveillance. It's like something out of *Lethal Weapon Four*." She shook her head. "Totally weird."

"They haven't caught him yet?" Christina asked, holding her breath.

"No. I wonder where he is. Probably left the state by now, don't you think?"

Christina was dying to confide in Randi, but she was afraid for Steve. Randi might not see things as she did and go to the police.

"Who knows," she murmured, looking out the window to avoid her friend's eyes.

"Well, I sure hope they get him soon." Randi sighed. "You know what I wish?"

"No," Christina answered hesitantly. "What?"

"I wish I could get out of school just for one day so I could hang out with you at the castle. You know, see what it's like being a soon-to-be-famous actress." She flopped on the bed and observed Christina through squinted eyes. "You're sort of like Jamie Lee Curtis."

"Huh?"

"Well, she got her start in horror films. Just think, someday you might have your own TV show!"

Christina sat beside her on the bed and cuddled her favorite teddy bear. He had white fur with a shiny black

130

nose and pink eyes. His name was Snowflake. She'd gotten him for her fifth birthday, and he never failed to comfort her.

Christina laughed. "TV show? Don't hold your breath. I may not live to be nineteen."

Randi stared at her, suddenly serious. "That pervert Jackson really has you scared."

"Whoever killed Amanda does—but it's not Steve."

Randi pushed up onto her elbow. "It's not?"

Christina swallowed. She had to talk to someone about Steve. If she couldn't trust Randi, who could she trust?

"No, it's not Steve. I saw him last night . . . and the night before."

Randi sucked in a sharp breath. "You lie!"

Christina shook her head. "Honest. He swore to me he had nothing to do with the answering-machine threat, the notes, or the bomb. He sort of, um . . . sort of likes me and has this silly collection of pictures in his locker— but that doesn't mean he's a nut case or that he'd murder me because I wouldn't go out with him." She stared down at her hands, amazed that she sounded so sure of herself. Her stomach was churning like a cement mixer.

"What are you thinking now?" Randi asked.

"Just that, well, he's different than I thought he'd be. Gentle . . . nice. Besides—" She grinned. "—he's cute."

"Fantastic!" Randi groaned. "Cute could kill!"

"Not Steve," Christina said firmly. "I thought about that all night long. If he'd wanted to kill me, he could have done it a dozen times. It would have been easy."

"But he didn't," Randi said thoughtfully.

"Right."

Her classmate pushed her plump body off the bed and worriedly paced the floor in front of Christina. "I don't know about this. If he's a couple of brain cells short, the stuff he does won't necessarily make sense. I read a book about serial killers. He could be waiting for a

131

special sign, a message from God or something. Then—whammo!—you're dead meat."

Christina shivered and bit down on her bear's ear. "I don't think so," she said after a moment's thoughtful fur-nibbling. "The trouble is, if it isn't Steve, it must be someone else who knows me awfully well. Someone who knew my schedule so they'd be sure I wouldn't be here, then they could leave a message on my machine. They also knew I wouldn't show up at my trailer while they were leaving the bookmark or writing the warning on my mirror."

"Someone who sees you every day," Randi murmured. "Probably someone on the movie set." She turned toward the window and stared out into the bright morning light.

"That's what Steve and I both think." Christina studied her friend, trying to see her as a stranger might.

Through all her ups and downs in modeling and acting, Randi had cheered her on. But it didn't stop there. Randi had written articles about her for the school newspaper. She had helped Christina shop for makeup and spectacular clothes at times she couldn't afford them for herself. When she hadn't been able to stick to her own diets, she had coached Christina through days of yogurt and nights of unbuttered popcorn—to make sure she could fit into a slinky dress she was supposed to model.

Any other girl might have been insanely jealous. But good old Randi never seemed to mind. And here she was again—plump, plain, but generous Randi, the true-blue, loyal friend. If Christina hadn't had her now, she didn't know what she'd do.

All that day, Christina struggled to concentrate on her lines, but her mind refused to cooperate. Again, she felt as if she were being watched. *Of course I'm being watched!* she told herself. After all, it took a couple of hundred people to make a movie. Because she was the costar, she'd naturally attract attention. Because everyone knew that someone was out to murder her, curiosity on the set tripled.

But this was different. What she felt was more like the sensation of being a hunted wild animal. She instinctively sensed that her life was in jeopardy.

As Kurt delivered his lines and the cameras rolled, she glanced at the plainclothesman who stood behind Dreising. It was Sergeant Mayhew again. She liked him. He seemed genuinely concerned about her.

Nevertheless, she felt restless. She longed to break loose from her keepers, to drive to the ocean and sit on the rocks, gazing at the surf. For a few hours, she just wanted to be like everyone else on the set, free to go anywhere she liked without fear of some lunatic following her.

One more minute of this, she thought, *and I'll scream!* She did.

"Cut! That was a great take, Chris. Very believable terror."

Dreising stepped across the tangle of cables and slung an arm companionably around her shoulders. Today he seemed a lot friendlier to her. Maybe there was a human bone in his body after all. Maybe losing Amanda had belatedly shocked him into understanding that people were real and precious.

"The rushes are looking super," he told her, referring to the unedited footage he and his film crew viewed at the end of each day. "You're going to look super up there on the big screen, sweetheart."

"If I survive," she muttered. She rarely felt sorry for herself, but she figured that this once she deserved the luxury.

Dreising laughed, tossing back his ponytailed head. Today he wore a Yankees T-shirt and a Red Sox baseball cap pulled down over his forehead, obscuring his eyes. She took back her thoughts of a moment earlier. He

133

looked more than ever like a wild kid who played a dangerous game.

Take number four—kill her right this time!

Christina shivered and shrugged off Dreising's arm.

"Hey, you *are* tense. Take it easy," he soothed. "This thing with Amanda has really got you spooked."

Christina looked him in the eye but said nothing.

"Hey, don't get me wrong," he said defensively. "I feel terrible about what happened to that poor girl. The world's a rough place sometimes. But we can't let some nut case stop us from doing what we love. Amanda wouldn't have wanted us to give up."

"That's what you told the press," Christina murmured.

"It's true. She was like that—anything for the show. Listen, any minute now the cops will nab the guy and dump him in some maximum-security hospital."

"I hope so."

Dreising looked thoughtful. "I have an idea. Why don't you go on back to your trailer. Take a nice long nap. We're shooting background shots all afternoon anyway."

"When will you need me?" Christina was aware of several people standing nearby, waiting to catch Dreising's attention. Among them were Beryl and her mother.

"I'm not sure." Dreising snatched a clipboard out of the hands of the young man who seemed to be acting as Amanda's replacement. The director studied his shooting schedule. "Tell you what—I'll send someone to wake you. We might try for a couple of night scenes after supper. If not, I'll see you in the morning."

"Okay," she answered, feeling a little better.

As Christina turned to leave, Mayhew followed a half dozen steps behind. Out of the corner of her eye, she could see Beryl's mother descending on Dreising. She thought about John again, and slowed down to watch his mother.

134

Seizing the director by the arm, Mavis demanded urgently, "Oh, Mr. Darling, I must have a word with you."

Dreising looked down his long nose at the immense woman standing before him in a garish orange dress that resembled a glow-in-the-dark tent. From the disgusted sneer on his face, she might have been a stray dog that was lifting its leg in his flower bed.

"It's Dreising," he informed her, "and I'm very busy, madam. See my assistant if you have a problem."

Christina hid an amused smile. She knew Mrs. Washington well enough to guess that, having once cornered Dreising, she wouldn't let him escape until she'd had her say.

"Wait!" Mavis Washington boomed, her eyes glowing with reckless purpose. "I've been talking to your crew . . . about the dailies—"

"They're called rushes now, Momma," Beryl corrected her, looking as if she wished she were dead. "Come on, leave Mr. Dreising alone."

Mavis shoved her daughter aside and blocked the director with her formidable body. "Everyone says Beryl looks wonderful in her scenes. She should have a much larger part, don't you agree? She's so very talented and—"

"*Mothe*r!" Beryl wailed, mortified.

Mavis swung a fat hand at her daughter, narrowly missing her cheek. "Shut up! Can't you see I'm trying to make you a star!" Turning back to Dreising, she smiled coquettishly at him, as if he hadn't heard what she'd just said. "Mr. Darling, sir, you know talent when you see it. All my little Beryl needs is the right break."

"She'll get a permanent one if you don't leave my set at once, lady!" Dreising roared. "Security! Where the hell are those idiots when you need them?"

This time Mrs. Washington has gone too far, thought Christina. Beryl was on the verge of tears and in danger of losing the modest role she had if her mother didn't back off fast.

Christina dashed over and stepped in front of the woman. "Mr. Dreising has a very tight shooting schedule," she explained as calmly as possible. "Maybe later he can think about other parts for Beryl. If you'll leave—"

"I won't!" Mrs. Washington stomped her foot like a child throwing a temper tantrum. "Not until he admits my Beryl's as good as some cheap little model! Better!" Her eyes narrowed to serpentine slits, focusing on Christina before moving on to Dreising. "How much did the Englishes pay you to give their daughter the starring role?"

Dreising snatched a walkie-talkie out of the hand of a nearby electrician. "Security!" he barked. "To the garden! Pronto!"

Sergeant Mayhew stepped closer to Christina, his eyes fixed intensely on Mavis Washington. "If we didn't already know who's been harassing you, I'd say we had a new suspect," he whispered.

"She's just a bad example of a stage mother," Christina commented.

Beryl must have overheard her. "You leave my mother out of this!" she snapped. "You'll never understand us because you're spoiled, Christina! You always get everything your way!"

Christina was taken by surprise. She'd been trying to help Beryl.

The girl gulped over huge tears, continuing to shout at Christina, "Everything! You fly all over the world, get paid thousands of dollars for wearing beautiful clothes. You even dumped my brother when you got too famous for a small-town boyfriend. And now this!" She gritted her teeth and glared at Christina with hatred pouring from her eyes.

"I—I'm sorry," Christina stammered.

Beryl dropped her face into her hands and sobbed.

"Come on," Mayhew said, steering Christina away. "Let her cool down. Your boss said you could go back to your trailer. Call your mom and dad to tell them you might be getting home late tonight, then take a break from these screwballs."

Feeling sorry for Beryl, Christina nodded and allowed the police officer to lead her away from the others. Before they'd gone far, she spotted John approaching at a run. Before she rounded the hedge, she saw him take his mother's arm and lead her away across the garden.

Christina climbed the steps to her trailer and reached absentmindedly for the door handle.

"Wait," Mayhew said, touching her shoulder to stop her from going inside. "Let me check first."

While he searched her dressing room, she glanced back over her shoulder toward the garden. Beryl's blow-up and Mavis's craziness gnawed at her. Then it struck her what had been most troubling about the emotional scene.

It was what Beryl had said about her having dumped John. How could she think such a terrible thing? She and John had dated for a while, sure, but it hadn't gotten serious. When they stopped going out, they'd remained friends.

Christina rubbed her forehead. A dull ache gathered behind her eyes. *Can you think of anyone who holds a grudge against you?* she remembered Lieutenant Draper asking.

But Beryl had always seemed the all-bark-no-bite type of person. Like her mother. Mrs. Washington was bossy and obnoxious, but she was basically harmless. Or was she?

When the cop returned and beckoned her inside, she asked, "Did you mean what you said about Mrs. Washington?"

Sergeant Mayhew stroked his mustache and considered her question. "About the woman being suspicious?"

"Yeah."

He nodded. "Her daughter's not exactly on terra firma either. If it makes you feel any better, I just called Lieutenant Draper and told him about the two of them. As soon as he gets a search warrant, he's sending a couple of men over to check out their house. Of course, we're ninety-nine percent sure it was that kid Steve. But on the off chance a stage mom would try to bump you off—" He winked at her, trying to ease her nervousness.

Christina worried her bottom lip between her teeth. "I think Beryl might be more of a threat than Steve," she said cautiously.

Mayhew frowned. "You really like that kid, don't you?"

She felt her cheeks heat up. "I guess so."

"Listen," he said, suddenly serious, "don't try to find someone to blame this on just to take the heat off of some guy you've got a crush on. There are plenty of nice boys with their heads screwed on straight who'd stop breathing for a date with a cover girl like you."

She nodded, holding back the tears. *Steve wouldn't stop breathing for me, because then he couldn't wrestle,* she thought.

And then she realized, maybe that was the one reason she liked him better than any other guy she'd met. Because there were things in his life just as important to him as acting and modeling were to her. Because, in spite of his photo collection, he didn't treat her like a trophy, he treated her like his equal. And that was terribly important to her.

"Dreising's right," Mayhew said, handing her a wad of Kleenex from the box on her dressing table—as if he knew she couldn't hold back her tears much longer. "Sleep for a while, you'll feel better. Who knows, maybe by the time you wake up, we'll have Jackson locked up."

Chapter 13

Surprisingly, when Christina awoke, she did feel a lot better. In fact, she felt as if she'd slept for hours. Her headache was gone. The tense knot in the bottom of her stomach had loosened. Lazily, she rolled onto her side and squinted at the dial of the tiny travel alarm on the shelf beside her cot.

"Eleven o'clock!" she gasped. She sat up and stared at the mini-blinds covering the windows. The cracks showed only black night outside.

Christina's breath came in shallow spasms. "Sergeant Mayhew?" she called softly.

No answer.

Of course, she thought, *by now he's been relieved by someone new*. But the other man should have answered her call.

Her hands shaking, she reached for her telephone and pressed the receiver to her ear as she quickly punched in numbers. Her hand froze midair. She hung up, picked up the receiver again.

"Oh, no," she breathed. No dial tone. The line was dead.

Unsure what to do now except get out of the trailer, Christina jumped off the cot, grabbed jeans and T-shirt, and shoved her feet into her already loosely laced tennis shoes.

Her heart thumping a warning tattoo in her chest, she carefully opened the trailer door and peered outside.

"Is anyone here?" she called, louder than before. "Hello?"

Perhaps her guard had left for just a moment to find a bathroom. He might be timid about coming in and using hers while she slept.

The cool, piney air soothed her with its familiar scent. But the darkness felt thick and dangerous.

Cautiously, Christina stepped down from the trailer and into the clearing.

She knew there would be a security guard somewhere on the lot all night long. He'd pass by the trailers once every hour or so. But it might be a long time before his next rounds.

She ran to the neighboring trailer—Kurt's—and rattled the door. It was locked. The one on the other side of hers was also bolted tight, and so was every other dressing room and office she tried. No telephones. No way to call for help.

The same feeling that had haunted her all day returned. Someone was watching her, perhaps amused at her dilemma, waiting for the perfect moment to . . .

No! She couldn't think like that. She'd only make her situation worse. The important thing was to find other people. She'd be safe as long as she wasn't alone. And if there were no others to protect her? Then she must somehow get to her car and drive home.

She looked up at the castle. Lights were on in the first floor and in the stone turret that rose another two floors above the third-floor roof. Perhaps Dreising was still filming inside. He'd said they might shoot late tonight.

Christina walked briskly into the garden that separated the trailers from the castle with its maze of paths and hedges. She hadn't gone more than twenty steps when she thought she heard stealthy footsteps echoing her own.

She stopped. Held her breath. Her heartbeat hammered so thunderously she could hear nothing else at first. Straining her ears, she detected the soft crunch of something moving through the nearby brush.

Christina broke into a run.

The path ahead wound through a labyrinth of six-foot hedges. She hesitated a split second, afraid to close herself off from view. But the footsteps following her had turned to a frantic thrashing through grass and shrubs, and she realized she had no choice but to plunge on.

She knew the paths by heart but hadn't gone far before her body reminded her how unused she was to running. A hot pain sliced through her ribs. Her breath ripped, shallow and sharp, through her lungs. Her legs felt like sacks of cement.

Ahead, the castle loomed loftily above the hedges. The lights in the windows gave her hope. If Dreising had kept even a skeleton crew late, she'd be safe among them. They'd watch out for her until her bodyguard returned.

Unless . . .

A terrible thought occurred to her.

If Dreising had, after all, been behind the notes, behind the bloody threat on her mirror and the letter bomb . . . If he had, as the police at first suspected, tried to scare up publicity for his film by creating a true-life horror story . . . then Dreising himself might be chasing her toward her death this very minute.

A frigid fear seeped into her bones. This afternoon the eccentric director had suggested that she take a nap in her trailer. Knowing how exhausted she was, how many nights she'd gone with too little sleep, he could have figured she'd sleep deeply. So deeply she wouldn't wake up unless someone woke her. Nightmarish pieces of the puzzle fell into place in her mind. Dreising had no intention of calling her for a late shoot. He'd dismissed his crew. He had her alone.

Despite the voice screaming in her brain, *Run! Run! Run!* she staggered to a halt and, clutching her side, gasped for air.

Branches crackled and creaked, as if her hunter were taking a shortcut through the hedge. The noise sounded close—almost on top of her—but she still couldn't see anything in the dark.

In spite of the agonizing pain shooting through her ribs, Christina forced herself to run again. To run for her life, her heart thundering in her ears, the sharp spring breeze howling through her hair.

She reached the castle, still unsure what to do next. She'd never make it to the parking lot and her car. And she'd told her parents she might be working late, so it would be hours before they'd worry about her. Then she remembered that John had told her that the ancient estate was riddled with tunnels and held dozens of rooms on the two floors above the one used for filming. If she could hide somewhere until morning when the cast and crew returned . . .

If I survive the night, Christina told herself, *I'll be okay.*

She shoved her shoulder into the heavy oak door, praying it would be unlocked. The splintery wood moved inward with a low groan, announcing her arrival. Without looking back to see how close her enemy might be, she dashed inside, then turned to lock it behind her.

"No!" she gasped. There was no bolt, only a huge keyhole. And she had no key.

The musty darkness in the great hall prickled her skin. She stifled the impulse to call out to whoever might still be around—because there was no way of knowing if she'd be summoning help or signaling her location to a killer.

Moving swiftly on tiptoe, she crossed the stone floor to the spiraling wooden staircase. The cupboard-like door beneath the steps led to a dank cellar where the bug man

142

had housed his creepy crawlies. She wondered if the bugs were still down there.

Not down. Definitely not down, she decided.

She started climbing the steps to the second floor.

Christina reached the first landing and heard the front door creak open again, then moan as it slowly closed. She pressed her back to the stone wall, breathing hard, listening. She heard the sizzle of a match being struck, then watched as the flat orange glow of candlelight crept up the stairway toward her.

An involuntary whimper of terror escaped her lips before she clamped her hand over her mouth. She flew up the staircase to the second floor and ran down a long, paneled hallway.

Dim rectangles of moonlight slanted through windows from the side rooms, lighting her way. She sensed that it would be only seconds before whoever chased her reached the top step and turned into the corridor. Then he'd spot her.

She ducked into the next room.

Luckily, it was one of the few that had been used to store props. Mammoth antique furniture offered several hiding places.

Christina decided that crawling under the four-poster bed would be too obvious. She fixed on the massive armoire, an old-fashioned wooden closet. No good. That would be one of the first places he'd search. Then she spotted a bureau that had been pushed into an alcove. Perhaps there was enough room to squeeze behind . . .

"Christina! I know you're in here!" a voice issued from the hallway.

She dove for the alcove, sucked in her breath, and forced herself into the narrow, cobwebby space behind the chest of drawers.

Holding her breath as she pressed her back against the cold stone wall, she listened to footsteps pause outside the doorway. Maybe he wouldn't realize which room she'd gone into. Maybe she was safe as long as . . .

The soft padding of rubber-soled shoes crossed the wood floor and stopped in the middle of the room. Her heart hammering in her chest, Christina slid down the wall. She peered cautiously around the corner of the bureau.

All she could make out in the faint splotches of moonlight was a pair of Reeboks with glow-in-the-dark patches on the heels. They moved stealthily across the floor toward the bed. Now she could see more of their owner. He was dressed in dark-colored sweatpants and jersey. His back to her, he crouched and lifted a corner of the tasseled spread to peer under the bed.

Thank you, she mouthed, her heart racing.

But he apparently wasn't satisfied.

Leaping to his feet, he flipped aside the heavy draperies, checking behind them. He yanked wide the mirrored armoire doors and riffled through the dresses hanging there, growing more and more agitated when he found nothing but costumes.

Go away! she prayed, panic rising inside her like a storm tide. She scrunched her eyes shut, her cheek pressed to the floor. *Oh, please, go away and leave me alone!*

When she opened her eyes, the tennis shoes stood within two feet of her nose. Christina blinked, dizzy with fear, her mouth dry with terror.

With unexpected strength her pursuer lifted the bureau out of the alcove, leaving her crouching helplessly on the floor before him.

She choked as she looked up into his face. "Steve?"

"What are you doing here?" he demanded in a hoarse whisper. Setting down the bureau, he seized her arm and pulled her to her feet.

"I—I . . ." She couldn't say what she was thinking. *So I was wrong and everyone else was right.* It was Steve all along. Steve had left the terrifying messages, had killed

144

an innocent woman with a bomb he'd made for *her*. And because she'd trusted him and ignored the advice of the police, she too was going to die at his hands.

"Stop looking at me that way!" he ground out, giving her a teeth-chattering shake.

She swallowed, unable to speak.

"Why did you come back here without your police escort?"

"Come back?" she asked, confused. By now he should have finished her off. Why prolong her agony with stupid questions?

"Yeah. Everyone left the lot long ago. So why'd you ditch your bodyguard and come back here alone?"

For the first time in the most nightmarish minutes of her life, she wondered if Steve might not intend to kill her after all.

"I fell asleep in the trailer," she explained shakily. "When I woke up everyone was gone."

Steve scowled skeptically at her.

"Honest. And Sergeant Mayhew was nowhere around."

"Why didn't you pick up the phone and call security?"

"The line was dead, and all the other trailers were locked."

"So you came here?"

Something suddenly struck her. "Where's the candle?" she asked.

"What candle?"

"The one you lit after you followed me into the castle," she reminded him impatiently.

Steve stared at her. "I don't understand, Chris. I never lit a candle," he whispered. "And . . . and I didn't follow you in here. I've been hiding here from the police the past couple of nights. I was in one of the bedrooms down the hallway when I heard you."

A terrible chill seized Christina. She wrapped her arms around her ribs to stop the shaking.

145

"What's wrong?" Steve asked.

"I . . . oh, Steve . . . someone's in here with us."

He looked into her eyes. "How—"

She pressed her fingertips over his lips and pulled him behind the open door so that they couldn't be seen from the hallway.

"Someone followed me from the trailer. I thought it was Dreising." Words tumbled out of her. "But now I'm not sure. It's all so confusing. I tried to get to my car, but he was catching up with me too fast. When I saw lights on in the castle, I figured I might be safe here."

He nodded, understanding. "The candle?"

"Whoever followed me lit a candle in the entryway and brought it with him up the stairs."

He looked around the room, a desperate expression in his eyes. "Geez! We've been wasting valuable time. Hold on." He stepped to one side and peered around the door into the hallway.

"What do you see?" she whispered.

"Light coming from a room two doors down," he whispered hoarsely. "Whoever's there must be working his or her way toward us. We have to move fast."

She swallowed. "Where?"

"Up. The next floor. With luck we can make it across the hall to the back stairway. It leads up to the servants' quarters."

Christina knew that if they made their dash at the wrong moment, they were dead. However, if they stayed where they were, they'd be dead a lot sooner.

"Now!" Steve hissed between his teeth and grabbed her hand.

Together they ran down the hallway and pushed through a narrow door into a dusky stairwell. *This must be the bottom of the turret*, she thought. Slits in the stone wall let in faint rays of moonlight. Stone steps corkscrewed upward around a central pillar.

"Go!" he ordered.

146

Christina climbed like lightning. Breathless, she pushed herself up the last few steps toward yet another door. As she threw herself forward, her hand extended toward the latch, she caught her toe on the top step.

A jagged flash of pain shot through her ankle, and she cried out before she could stop herself.

"What's wrong?" Steve asked, his face pinched with fear.

"My ankle. I twisted it."

"Can you walk?"

"I don't know. I can try."

Christina braced herself against the stone wall and hobbled up the last step and through the door. The third floor hadn't been open to the public or used during the filming. In fact, dense tents of cobwebs suggested it had been a long time since anyone had set foot here.

"Amanda told the cast that we weren't to come up here," she whispered. "The floor is rotting."

"We don't have any choice," Steve gasped.

She nodded. "Which way?"

"Doesn't matter. Stay close to the wall. The floor might be more stable there."

Steve wrapped an arm around her to help her limp faster. He passed the first two rooms, apparently wanting to put more distance between them and the back stairwell. If they chose a room in the center of the hall, two exits would be equally close. Or equally far away, she thought.

The room they entered was empty except for a mound of metal bed frames and mildewing mattresses in the middle of the floor.

"Cozy," Steve commented dryly.

Christina's stomach dropped to her knees. "There's no place to hide in here."

He looked around frantically. Then a determined light flashed in his dark eyes. "There's only one thing we can do. I'll try to draw the creep away from you. If I make it out of the castle, he'll follow, but I'm sure I can outrun him. I'll head for the security shack and bring help."

He grabbed a leg of one bed and lifted the heavy frame with effort. "Hide under here. It's the only place there is."

She stared at the tangle of springs and tattered mattresses. Surprisingly, the trash heap provided decent camouflage. Crouching, she crawled under the frame and wriggled herself into a space beneath one of the mattresses. It smelled like rodent droppings and putrefied cotton.

Steve gently lowered the metal frame. Her ankle throbbed wickedly, but, other than that, she wasn't uncomfortable.

"You okay?" he whispered.

"Yes. Hurry," she pleaded.

"I will," he promised. Bending down, he kissed her lightly on the lips. "I'll be back as fast as I can. Promise."

Chapter 14

Steve peered into the hallway. A sinister orange glow filtered up the back stairwell he and Christina had climbed moments earlier. If he ran like hell, he could make it down the main staircase and out the front door ahead of whoever stalked Chris. He felt sure that if he could just sit down and calmly think about everything that had happened, he could figure out who it was. But this was no time to wrestle with suspects and motives, and he didn't dare risk lagging behind to catch a glimpse of Chris's pursuer.

Steve waited until the light almost reached the hallway. If whoever carried that candle saw him just as he disappeared around the corner and down the stairs, it might look as if Christina were ahead of him. He was betting the killer would follow.

"Hurry! Run!" he shouted convincingly, as he tore around the curved banister and crashed down the stairs.

He didn't dare glance backward even for an instant. One misstep on the ancient boards and he'd tumble to the bottom.

Jumping the last three steps, Steve raced across the great hall and hit the front door at top speed. In a flash of panic, he imagined the door locked and himself cornered, but it creaked open willingly in his hand. Then he was outside in the dewy night, released from the evil of the castle.

Gulping down lungfuls of fresh air, Steve sprinted across the deserted movie lot. He kicked at cables, clunked into lighting tripods, and rammed dollies, intentionally making as much noise as he could to draw attention to his flight. With any luck the clamor would also roust the guard.

"Hey! Anyone here?" he shouted. "Security! Security, where are you?"

But he got no answer.

At last, he slowed and dared to glance behind him. No one. No one was there.

He stopped running to better listen, wiping the flow of perspiration from his brow with the sleeve of his sweatshirt. There was only the rasping sound of his own breathing, the innocent flutter of a spring breeze through dark tree limbs overhead. The air smelled of spring buds and moist earth—a pretty night if Death hadn't been stalking.

Breaking into a run again, he made it to the guard shack at the lower end of the parking area.

"Hey! Guard, where the hell are you?"

No one seemed to be around. The guy could have been out on the lot or curled up in one of the trailers, asleep. Furious, he let himself into the unlocked shed, grabbed the telephone, dialed 911—and only belatedly realized that the line was dead.

A sickening sensation filled his stomach. *It isn't just Christina's phone. He's cut the main line.*

His mind racing in useless circles, Steve stared at the clock above the guard's desk. *Midnight. Five hours before any of the crew arrives.* He swallowed and blinked, realizing their chances of surviving those five hours weren't very good. He had to get Christina away from here. But how could he when she was unable to run?

150

The solution came to him all at once. A weapon. He needed a weapon to defend himself and her. He tore open desk drawers, scrambled through the contents of the guard's closet, hoping to find a gun. There was none. What now?

Props! he thought. On a horror-movie set where actors threatened one another with everything from axes to blowguns, he ought to be able to find some kind of weapon. He remembered the inside of Gus's trailer, crammed with special-effects gadgets. With any luck, he'd find what he needed there.

Tearing out of the shed, he ran back across the parking lot, empty except for Christina's car. No one seemed to be following him, but that realization gave him only a moment's relief. If he'd lost the guy, that must mean he'd given up on Steve and returned to search for Christina.

Realizing he had only minutes, Steve at last reached Gus's trailer. He pulled on the door. It was locked.

Steve groaned aloud with frustration. He examined the latch. Cheap and breakable . . . if he could lay his hands on something with which to force it. But he didn't have time to hunt up tools. He circled around to the back and found a low window. Lifting out the screen, he tossed it on the ground, then found a good, hefty rock and heaved it at the glass.

The pane shattered loudly. He pulled off his shirt. Wrapping it around his hand to protect the skin, he broke out jagged pieces of glass clinging to the frame, then eased himself through and into the dark trailer. He had to chance turning on a light to see.

His fondest wishes came true. The rear end of the makeup man's trailer looked like a small arsenal. Pistols, swords, daggers, hand grenades, wires, and detonators— a selection from the studio's vast collection of prop weapons. Hadn't he read somewhere that Dreising had been an FX man before he'd started directing? The guy was so fond of gadgets and dramatic scenes he often wrote extra stunts into the script on the day of shooting. It looked as if Gus had come prepared for anything.

Steve scanned the small rack of firearms. He'd seen enough movies to identify most of them—an Uzi, two 45's, a double-barreled shotgun, an army-issue M-16. He supposed they were real, but fired blanks for the purpose of filming. He'd shot his father's target pistol before. Never anything more powerful. He selected a dull-gray automatic handgun from the rack, grabbed a box of shells, then, as an afterthought, a couple of other items that might prove useful.

Christina willed her body to shrink within her tomb of springs and mattresses. She felt like a little kid playing a deadly game of hide-and-seek. Back when she was seven or eight years old, when it came time to choose a hiding place, she'd always panicked. Behind the stairs was too open. In the basement—too closed off, only one way out. The attic was ridiculously obvious and spooky besides. When she'd reluctantly chosen a spot and waited, holding her breath, pressing her hands to her chest to quiet her heart, she'd always known she would be found. It was a horrible feeling.

But then it had just been a game. This was for real. "It" was a murderer.

She became aware of the muffled sound of steps outside the doorway. She hadn't heard anyone on the stairs after Steve had made his noisy exit.

Sucking air between her teeth, she squeezed her eyes closed to steady her nerves. Whoever it was, she must keep her cool, remain absolutely still. He or she would look into the room, see bare walls, no furniture, a jumble of old springs and tattered mattress dumped in the middle of the floor. And leave.

She opened her eyes . . . and her jaw dropped in a silent gasp of horror. The creature that walked into the dark room wasn't human.

Its face had caved in around the skull, tatters of flesh hanging from chalky bones. One eyeball had been gouged out, leaving gory trails of veins and ligaments in its place.

She bit down on her fist as the thing plodded across the room, raising a candle to light its way. It was tall, she noticed, and slim. In fact, too tall and slight to be Dreising, she realized.

The creature turned and considered the pile of broken beds. It set a brass candle holder on the floor and reached out to pull back one corner of a mattress. Curiously, it peered into the metal web concealing Christina.

She froze, staring up into its one good eye, unable to tell if the thing saw her or—as long as she didn't move— if she seemed part of a pattern of shadows.

That gross face, she thought, *I've seen it before*. She caught a whiff of dried latex . . . then she knew. Gus's trailer. Her enemy wore one of a set of full-face masks Gus had made of Sir Neville in his advanced zombie state.

Slowly the masked head drew back, and the person wearing it straightened.

He's leaving! Christina thought, the corners of her lips lifting into a half-smile.

Without warning, the creature whirled around. A furious snarl escaped his lips as he grasped the top bed frame and tossed it aside. Knowing it would be seconds before he cast aside the mattress that was the only object between them, Christina crawled free from the opposite end and hobbled on her injured leg toward the door.

He was much faster.

Strong arms clasped around her waist, picked her up, and heaved her against the wall. Her head struck stone, stunning her. She pressed her palms to her temples, desperately trying to calm the dizziness, to gather her wits so that she'd know what to do.

153

But he was on her again, dragging her to her feet by her shirt and forcing her against the wall. The gruesome face pinched and wheezed as its wearer moved his mouth inside.

"You'll pay!" he snarled. "You spoiled witch, you'll die!"

Through a spinning fog, Christina remembered something she'd learned during a rehearsal for a play. Her role required that she fend off a would-be rapist.

She jerked a knee sharply upwards, catching Sir Neville in the groin.

He let out a bellow of pain and dropped her.

Scrambling on all fours, she slipped from between him and the wall, then got onto her good foot and limped from the room.

Christina looked desperately up and down the dark hallway, knowing she'd bought herself only a few seconds. Steve was nowhere in sight, and she didn't hear him coming. In fact, she had no way of knowing if her assailant had gotten to Steve before he'd been able to find help.

Despair filled her at the thought that Steve might be hurt or worse, but she forced herself to hobble toward the rear stairwell. *Down*, she told herself, *go down*. Heroines in horror movies were always so dumb. They ascended endless flights of stairs to spooky attics, where they knew there was no way out. By going down she might, with luck, escape the castle. Maybe by now the security guard was close enough to hear her screams and come to investigate.

She'd descended six steps in the tightly winding stairwell when she came to a dead stop.

Jammed in the narrow well below her was a pile of old furniture. He'd blocked her off. Her only chance now was to continue up inside the turret.

Feeling doomed, Christina climbed the stairs, her ankle threatening to give out on every step.

Behind her, she could hear a door open and close. She froze, hoping he hadn't seen her enter the stairwell. Hoping he'd think she'd headed for the main staircase.

There was a pause. Then the steps started upwards, following her . . . and she had no choice but to climb higher.

At the top of the stairs, she found a wooden trapdoor. It was riddled with wormholes and creaked in protest when she pushed upwards against it. Being quiet no longer mattered. She shoved with all her strength, and the door flopped open with a bang.

Pulling herself up through it, she glanced around. The room was round, with wide slots in the stone for windows but no glass. A cold wind blew off the river, tearing at her hair.

Where are you, Steve? Please hurry! she prayed. Then, having nowhere to go, she spun around to face Sir Neville.

To her surprise, when he came up the stairs he was holding a copy of the film script and a pen. Hysterically, she thought, *What does he want, an autograph?* She backed up as far as she could, pressing her shoulder blades against the rough granite.

He spotted her immediately, and smiled as best as the mask allowed. "Good. Very good," he muttered.

The voice sounded oddly familiar but pitched too high.

"What do you want from me?" Christina demanded, the words grating in her throat.

"Write," he said.

"A suicide note?" In spite of her terror, a laugh bubbled up inside of her. "No one would ever believe I killed myself."

"Not suicide. A clue for the police, to help them find your killer."

She glared at him, feeling braver now that she had nothing left to lose. "Like he's a guy, about six feet tall with large hands, dark hair, and brown eyes?"

The eyes blinked warily through the mask holes.

"I can see the hair on your wrists," she explained. "And making your voice sound squeaky is a rotten imitation of a girl."

"You always were a show-off, Christina," he growled, his voice suddenly an octave lower. "Well, that was your last shot." He turned the script over so that the blank backs of the pages faced up and thrust it at her. "Write what I tell you."

Her hand shaking, she slowly reached out for the pen. *Kill time*, her brain warned her. *Do what he says but in slow motion. Someone has to come. Please God, make them come soon!*

He cleared his throat. "Write 'If anything happens to me tonight, arrest Steve Jackson. He came to my house last night. I felt sorry for him, but I think I made a mistake.'"

"If any . . . thing . . . happens to . . . me—What comes next?" she asked innocently.

From beneath his shirt, Sir Neville pulled out a long, shiny blade. "You know what I said. Write faster or I'll throw you off the turret without putting you out of your misery first."

Christina wrote the rest hastily, knowing there was nothing more she could do to stall him. She still wouldn't go without a fight, but given the fact he was much bigger and stronger than she was, it couldn't last long.

He took the letter from her and read it silently. "Good, very good." Then, clasping the mask beneath the chin, he peeled it up and over his head.

"John!" she gasped.

"You must have known it was me," he snarled over a curled lip. "The mask was more for Steve's sake than yours. He'll walk away alive tonight, but won't get far. The cops already figure he was behind the threats and letter bomb. In the morning, when they find your body at the base of the turret and this note in your trailer, they'll be sure he's their man."

"But why?" Christina choked out, tears flooding her eyes. "Why would you do this to me?"

He shook his head in disbelief. "Why? The real question should be *why not*—after everything you've done to me and my family."

She scowled, still not understanding.

"You destroyed my sister's acting career. You hurt my mother. And you dumped me! That was the worst, Christina. We were super together. Really great. The perfect couple. But you were selfish. You figured I wasn't good enough for you."

"No!" she cried. "It wasn't like that at—"

He ignored her denial. "I bet you wanted Kurt to fall for you. Boy, that would have been a feather in your cap! Is he the kind of guy you were waiting for? I'm surprised Steve even bothered with you, as rotten as you treated him."

"I didn't mean to hurt anyone!" Christina cried. "I swear, John, I didn't. I was just . . . just trying to be the best at what I always wanted to be—an actress. I didn't have time for dating, boyfriends, and parties. I was always working."

He laughed bitterly. "You call that working? Working is waiting tables in some scummy restaurant, like my mom does to feed us. Working is doing all the stupid, dirty jobs on a movie set that are beneath some hotshot director and his spoiled cast."

She reached out for him. "I'm sorry, John. Please believe me. I didn't mean to—"

His face stiffened as he snapped his arm away from her. "It's too late. I can't change my plans now. You know about me, and you'll tell."

It was useless to lie.

"If you stop now, though, maybe it won't go so hard on you. Maybe a good lawyer could convince the jury that the letter bomb was just a prank that went wrong."

"Fat chance."

"Please!" she whimpered as he started toward her, the dagger raised in his hand, his eyes gleaming with evil purpose.

"Listen to her!" a voice barked out from the door-way.

John whipped around.

"You!" he growled, his eyes widening as he spotted the gun in Steve's hand. A nervous grin spread across his lips. "So, you decided to play rough, too."

"If I have to, I will," Steve ground out.

Christina drew her tongue over fear-parched lips. How had Steve found a gun so fast?

John must have been thinking the same thing. "Gus's props," he chuckled. "Very good. I hope you realize that the only ammo he keeps is blanks. Think you're gonna scare me away with a big bang?"

Steve didn't blink. He looked as fierce and determined as if he were facing down a wrestling opponent on the mat. "You're wrong. This one's loaded with the real stuff."

Christina backed away. "Steve—"

He didn't seem to hear her. "Give it up, John. Even if I didn't have the gun, you know you can't beat me if we go one on one."

Christina knew that he wasn't just bragging. In a wrestling match between the two boys, Steve, the state champ, would pin John in seconds. But John was too smart to let that happen. He was keeping his distance, circling the walls of the curved tower chamber as Steve spoke.

"Come down with me to the guard shack. We'll wait there for the police. You can't kill again and get away with it."

"Watch me." With a wicked flash in his eyes, John lunged for Christina.

She leaped away, the blade of his knife grazing her arm.

Instead of shooting. Steve reached out to try to intercept John with his free hand. But the other boy surprised him by changing direction and grabbing for the gun.

Knocking the pistol out of Steve's grip with one hand, John dropped the knife and landed a fierce left cross in his stomach. Steve doubled over, gasping for air. John dove for the gun as it skittered across the splintery floor. And so did Christina.

Their hands reached the pistol at the same second.

"No!" she screamed.

She had no idea whether the pistol was loaded with blanks or real cartridges, but she wasn't willing to risk her and Steve's life on it.

She gripped the gun's handle. John seized the muzzle and twisted while prying her fingers loose with his other hand. Pain shot up through her arm as something snapped in her hand. With a cry of defeat, she lost her hold.

John swung the weapon around. As Steve at last straightened up, recovering from the blow to his gut, John aimed at his chest.

Christina saw the look of horror on Steve's face and realized the awful truth. He was afraid because he knew. He knew what he'd loaded that gun with.

"Don't do it, John!" Steve warned. "You'll spend your life in prison."

John sneered, "No way, man. Who's gonna tell what really happened tonight? Not you, Jackson—you're a sicko fan who's been stalking Christina. You corner her, she shoots you in self-defense, then trips on the rotting stairs while running from the tower. That's the story I'll give the cops . . . if they don't figure it out for themselves." He grinned.

"John!" Christina screamed as she watched his finger slowly squeeze the trigger.

A loud crack reverberated through the stone tower, then a second. For a moment, Steve stood, looking stunned, then his hands clutched his chest and he grimaced.

When he removed his hands and stared down at his chest, a vicious crimson stain had already begun to spread across his sweatshirt.

"Oh, Steve—" Christina cried. "No. Oh, please, no."

John broke out in a demonic laugh. "Son of a gun, it wasn't blanks after all. You meant to shoot me dead! Amazing how fast the tables turn, ain't it, Jackson?"

Steve dropped to his knees, his jaw working, eyes wide with pain. Blood seeped from the corners of his lips. He collapsed face-down on the floor, his forehead striking the floor with a resounding thump.

Ignoring John, Christina ran to Steve. She tried to turn him over, but he was as heavy as a lead statue.

John pulled her off and onto her feet.

She looked up into his dark eyes, hating him more than she'd ever hated anyone in her life. "Why?" she shrieked, tears streaming down her cheeks.

"Because he wouldn't quit," John stated simply. "It was him or me."

He stuck the pistol into his belt. Twisting one of her arms behind her back, he walked her toward the stairwell.

With a fierce shove, John forced her to the edge of the top step. Christina's injured ankle gave way, and she crumpled to the floor.

"Get up!" John roared.

She glanced futilely around the turret, settling on Steve's body. He'd died trying to protect her. But now was not the time to mourn him. Her own survival was still at stake.

Between the top step where she sat and Steve's body was the carved stone balcony she'd often seen from below—the one that had caused the crew to rope off a section of the patio below because chunks of mortar and stone frequently fell from the jutting platform. The structure was supported by wooden braces, but she suspected that they weren't very strong. Any additional

160

weight might bring the whole balcony down. It was a five-story drop.

Christina glanced up at John. "My ankle must be sprained. I can't stand on it."

"You won't have to for long. Quit stalling. Get up!"

As Christina started to stand, she took John by surprise, dropping one shoulder and rolling across the floor the way she'd seen stunt people do in dozens of movies to escape a speeding car or stampeding horses. Right away she could feel the stone structure shiver beneath her. She pressed herself against the wall as half the balcony broke off and fell away. She watched it go, as if in slow motion, tumbling slowly away from her. It struck the paved patio below with a deafening crash and exploded into dust.

Just like my skull will when I—

John peered onto the balcony, being careful not to set foot on it. His eyes gleamed with anticipation.

"It won't work, Christina," he gloated. "Doesn't matter whether you fall down the stairs or off a balcony. The cops will figure you fired those shots into Steve as you were going over the edge."

"I won't jump!" she shouted at him. "You're going to have to push me. And if you get near enough to push me, I'll take you with me, John Washington. I swear I will."

At first he looked surprised, then a resigned calm spread across his dull eyes, and he boldly stepped onto the balcony.

There was nowhere for Christina to go. She could feel the stonework vibrating ominously as John's weight was added to hers.

Chunks of mortar from the underside cracked away and smashed on the patio.

"It's over!" he shouted, rushing at her.

Christina felt the world sway as the stone floor dropped away beneath them. She grabbed for John, but he

161

was intent upon staying out of her reach. Her hand struck something solid, and she reflexively clung to it. As she jerked to a halt, a scream of shock and agony whooshed past her in the night. From below, she heard a hollow thud.

Christina shut her eyes as silence closed around her. She hadn't the strength to pull herself up.

"Chris!" a voice rang out. "Chris, where are you?"

Astonished, she looked up, past her white knuckles that were wrapped around a rusty iron support extending through the broken mortar. "Steve? Is that you?"

"Yeah."

She was dreaming. She *had* to be dreaming. But, just to be sure: "Don't come out here! The balcony's gone."

He appeared in the turret doorway. The bloodstain covering most of his chest was still fresh. She didn't understand how he could have come back to life, but she didn't ask any questions as he stretched out on his stomach and grabbed her wrist.

"Let go of the metal," he told her. "Trust me. I won't let you fall."

She glanced down again. In the pale morning light she could see John's body, at rest in a grotesquely distorted posture.

She shut her eyes and relaxed her fingers. Steve lifted her up over the jagged edge and quickly rolled them both into the sturdy turret.

Tears of relief flooded her eyes. Steve put his arms around her, and she rested her head on his shoulder as he stroked her hair.

"It's all right, Chris. You don't have to be brave any longer."

Chapter 15

Christina looked up from the red punch in the paper cup Steve handed her.

"Thanks," she said, smiling.

"Congratulations!" Steve raised his cup in a toast to her. "Your first movie is behind you. What do you think you'll do next? Another horror flick?"

"Not likely," Randi said, laughing.

She had been out of town for the past three weeks, helping her grandmother while she recuperated from surgery on her hip. Christina was thrilled that she'd been able to return in time to join her for the cast party in the garden of the state park. During her absence, the remaining scenes of *Dark Memories* had finally been shot, without any more accidents. The film was, as Dreising had put it, "in the can."

"You're right," Christina agreed, taking a bite of cake. "I'm going to stay away from horror films."

A local bakery had made the cake in the shape of a castle with ghoulish monsters peeping through its windows. Although the gray frosting looked sort of gross, it tasted great. Especially to someone who only a few weeks ago was sure she'd never eat, walk, or breathe again.

Christina glanced across the crowded garden at Dreising. The director was wearing a Minnesota Twins cap today. He and Kurt were deep in discussion. Probably planning a new movie, she thought. She hoped it wouldn't include her.

Kurt had behaved himself during the shooting of the rest of the film. He was dating one of the young women who worked with Gus Murphy. Once Kurt realized Christina really did have a boyfriend—who happened to be six feet tall, was built like a brick wall, and was a championship wrestler—he'd gracefully given up the chase.

If your fans only knew what a big chicken you are, Kurt Richmond. Christina mused, smiling to herself.

On the other hand, she considered Steve the bravest boy she'd ever known. He had risked his life for her. She smiled up at him as she licked the last few sugary crumbs of cake from her fingertips. Tossing her paper plate into the trash can, she slid her hand into his. He didn't seem to mind that her fingers were still a little sticky.

"So," Randi said, her sharp eyes missing nothing, "while I was gone, I read all about what happened in the paper. But none of the articles really explained why John was out to get you, Chris."

Christina's party mood slipped a notch. Even now, the mention of John's name made her nervous. She had to remind herself that he was dead and couldn't hurt her anymore. But the more she talked about what had happened, the easier it would become to deal with the lingering terror, and believe that it was over.

Christina studied her toes between the straps of her sandals, then looked up at Randi. "I wish we could have at least talked on the phone—but you know my dad and long-distance calls." She shrugged. "The police think that John wasn't just trying to get back at me for breaking up with him. He also had this crazy idea that if he eliminated me, Beryl would get my part in the film."

"You're kidding," Randi breathed.

Christina shook her head. "Actually, that wasn't very likely. The film was already in progress. Dreising would have needed someone with a lot more experience to pick up my role midstream. And he'd probably want someone who looked like me, so he could use some of the footage already shot. From a distance or the back, another blonde about my build and height, in my costume, could be made to look like me."

"And I thought he was so nice," Randi groaned.

Steve gave a humorless snort. "I talked to Sergeant Mayhew today. His theory is that John started out trying to scare Chris with a couple of pranks—the phone call, the note, and fake blood on the mirror. When John was told to drill holes in the casket Dreising planned to bury Chris in, he conveniently forgot. But nothing worked. Then he got serious about his game."

Christina took a deep breath to chase away the shiver Steve's words had sent through her. "John may have told himself that he was scaring me off the film for Beryl's sake, but I think he was trying to pay me back for breaking up with him."

"Blowing you up seems like overkill to me," Randi remarked dryly.

Steve looked at Christina, then Randi. "The police think the letter bomb was supposed to be more like a firecracker. They found library books on pyrotechnics and the activities of terrorist groups in John's room. My guess is, he was trying to design a fan letter that would make a really big bang, maybe burn Chris's fingers. He expected that would be the last straw. Chris would panic and quit the film."

Christina swallowed hard. "But he made the explosive charge much too strong. It would have killed me, like it did Amanda."

Randi looked suddenly pale. She cleared her throat. "The newspaper said there was a gun?"

"John didn't come gunning for me," Christina said. "He intended to push me off the castle turret and make it look like Steve did it. When he overheard Dreising telling me to take a nap, he knew he'd found a way to get me alone. Later that afternoon, when Dreising asked him to go to my trailer and let me know I wouldn't be needed until the next day, John only pretended to do it. Then he returned to Dreising and told him that he'd sent me home."

Randi looked thoughtful. "But why did he wait until so late to go after you?"

"The crew was shooting scenes inside the castle until after ten o'clock that night. He couldn't do anything until they left."

"And the gun?" Randi repeated.

"John didn't bring the pistol, I did," Steve stated. "See, we couldn't find the security guard. It turned out that he was catching a nap in one of the trailers. And John had cut the main phone line into the park, then knocked out Chris's bodyguard."

"Our only chance was to find a weapon fast," Christina put in. "But all the cartridges in the FX supplies were blanks."

"Right," Steve continued. "I figured that John would know that—but if I could distract him somehow I still might take him by surprise. I grabbed a blood bag and gel capsules from Gus's trailer along with the pistol and blanks. If John didn't swallow the real-gun ploy, I'd arrange to lose the gun to him in a fight. He'd shoot me. I'd play dead just long enough for him to let down his guard. Then I'd deck him and get Chris out of there."

"But something went wrong," Christina added with a mysterious smile.

Randi's eyebrows rose. "What?" she breathed.

Gently, Christina lifted a lock of dark hair off Steve's broad forehead. The remnants of a nasty bruise still marred his tan skin.

"I hit my head when I fell," he admitted sheepishly. "That wasn't part of my plan. I don't remember a thing until I heard Chris screaming."

She smiled up at him sweetly. "Next time you decide to rescue me, please don't wait until I'm hanging by my fingertips, five floors above a stone patio."

"Next time?" he teased. "Think you'll run into more crazed fans?"

"I hope not—but if I do, will you be around?"

"Definitely," he promised, squeezing her tightly. "Not only that, I'll be your personal exercise trainer. I hear every star has one these days. I'll whip you into shape." His cheeks flushed. "I mean . . . well, even better shape than you're in."

Christina grinned, feeling like the luckiest girl in the world. She'd dared to dream and take on tough challenges. Now she had her career, a loyal friend, and a great guy. What more could a girl ask for?